ROLLING THUNDER

Prophet and Brennan wrestled for the gun, the stage swerving this way and that across the trail. Brennan flicked the hammer back and twisted the Navy Colt toward Prophet's ribs.

Knowing he was about two seconds from having daylight carved through his middle, Prophet heaved on the gun with all his strength. He felt Brennan's wrist give. Prophet twisted the man's hand toward Brennan's own ribs.

"Noooooo!" Brennan raged, watching the barrel snug up against his bloodstained shirt. Prophet squeezed the man's hand until Brennan's index finger compressed the trigger. The gun barked and jumped. Brennan jerked, stiffened. His eyes glazed as his face blanched.

Jerking the man's gun from his slack hand, Prophet tugged his collar, rolling Brennan's lifeless body off the stage. He watched the hardcase sail down and back, hit the ground, bounce, and roll into the brush along the trail.

PRAISE FOR

PETER BRANDVOLD:

"Takes off like a shot, never giving the reader a chance to set the book down."
—Douglas Hirt

Berkley titles by Peter Brandvold

THE DEVIL'S LAIR
.45-CALIBER FURY
STARING DOWN THE DEVIL
.45-CALIBER REVENGE
THE DEVIL GETS HIS DUE
ONCE LATE WITH A .38
RIDING WITH THE DEVIL'S MISTRESS
ONCE UPON A DEAD MAN
DEALT THE DEVIL'S HAND
ONCE A RENEGADE
THE DEVIL AND LOU PROPHET
ONCE HELL FREEZES OVER
ONCE A LAWMAN
ONCE MORE WITH A .44
BLOOD MOUNTAIN
ONCE A MARSHAL

Other titles

DAKOTA KILL
THE ROMANTICS

THE
DEVIL'S LAIR

PETER BRANDVOLD

BERKLEY BOOKS, NEW YORK

THE BERKLEY PUBLISHING GROUP
Published by the Penguin Group
Penguin Group (USA) Inc.
375 Hudson Street, New York, New York 10014, USA
Penguin Group (Canada), 10 Alcorn Avenue, Toronto, Ontario M4V 3B2, Canada
(a division of Pearson Penguin Canada Inc.)
Penguin Books Ltd., 80 Strand, London WC2R 0RL, England
Penguin Group Ireland, 25 St. Stephen's Green, Dublin 2, Ireland (a division of Penguin Books Ltd.)
Penguin Group (Australia), 250 Camberwell Road, Camberwell, Victoria 3124, Australia
(a division of Pearson Australia Group Pty. Ltd.)
Penguin Books India Pvt. Ltd., 11 Community Centre, Panchsheel Park, New Delhi—110 017, India
Penguin Group (NZ), Cnr. Airborne and Rosedale Roads, Albany, Auckland 1310, New Zealand
(a division of Pearson New Zealand Ltd.)
Penguin Books (South Africa) (Pty.) Ltd., 24 Sturdee Avenue, Rosebank, Johannesburg 2196,
South Africa

Penguin Books Ltd., Registered Offices: 80 Strand, London WC2R 0RL, England

This is a work of fiction. Names, characters, places, and incidents either are the product of the
author's imagination or are used fictitiously, and any resemblance to actual persons, living or dead,
business establishments, events, or locales is entirely coincidental. The publisher does not have any
control over and does not assume any responsibility for author or third-party websites or their
content.

THE DEVIL'S LAIR

A Berkley Book / published by arrangement with the author

PRINTING HISTORY
Berkley edition / June 2005

Copyright © 2005 by Peter Brandvold.
Cover design by Steven Ferlauto.
Cover illustration by Guy Deel.

ISBN: 0-425-20384-0

BERKLEY®
Berkley Books are published by The Berkley Publishing Group,
a division of Penguin Group (USA) Inc.,
375 Hudson Street, New York, New York 10014.
BERKLEY is a registered trademark of Penguin Group (USA) Inc.
The "B" design is a trademark belonging to Penguin Group (USA) Inc.

PRINTED IN THE UNITED STATES OF AMERICA

10 9 8 7 6 5 4 3 2 1

For Mike and Madeline,
and Lucy and Bob

1

"RIDIN' THAT STAGE down there's the ugliest woman I ever laid eyes on," said Nasty Turk Mahoney. "I seen her when she boarded in Rosehawk."

"Ugly, eh?" said Jethro Hall, grinning around a chewed cigar.

"So ugly, she'd make a freight train take a dirt track."

"Big, mean-lookin', and hairy," Jubal Maguire added grimly, hunkered over his saddle horn. "I seen her too."

The men and three other hardcases sat their horses on the wooded ridge, staring north along the valley below.

A stagecoach had just come into view, moving west behind a six-horse team. From this distance, the red Concord coach was little more than an oval speck trailing a blond dust cloud. Its path through the sage-tufted canyon rimmed with towering pines would bring it to a point just below the ridge.

The six well-armed riders in dusters, soiled hats, and black bandannas stared like hunting hawks while their horses stomped impatiently, twitched their ears, and swished their tails at gnats.

Mike Ensor adjusted his two-hundred-plus pounds on his silver-trimmed saddle, spit a quid of chew on a fir tree, and crinkled his tiny eyes at Nasty Turk Mahoney.

"It ain't right to call a woman ugly," Ensor growled, his jowls turning red. "How'd you like it if someone called your ma ugly?"

Smirking, Mahoney turned his one-eyed gaze to Ensor. Mahoney's own face looked as though it had been hacked apart by Apache tomahawks and sewn back together by drunken army medicos. "My ma *was* ugly. I got my good looks from my pa." He chucked himself under his chin, his chapped, scaly lips shaping a grin.

Ensor stared at him, his doughy cheeks bunched with seething anger. "It ain't right, callin' a woman ugly." His voice was as taut as a dead man's noose.

"Lookit you, Mike," Mahoney taunted. "Why, an idiot as big and plug-ugly as you'd have to have a ma even uglier than mine. I bet plenty of people called her ugly. Probably called you ugly too—ain't that right, 'Little Mike'?"

Ensor's soft, round face turned a deep russet from his triple chin to the brim of his broad, black hat.

Mahoney held his stare with a mocking smile. "Fat and ugly shittin' out fat an' ugly." He shook his head. "Should be a law against it."

"Is that why you killed her, Little Mike?" J.D. Brennan asked, holding his double-barreled shotgun snug against his hip and looking on with amusement. "'Cause she passed on her ugly features?"

Ensor switched his acrimonious gaze to the stocky Brennan. Slowly, his fat, sunburned hand slid up his thigh to the long-barreled Smith & Wesson on his hip.

"All right, that's enough!"

The gang leader, Pike Thorson, rode up on his Appaloosa and swatted Little Mike with his soiled planter's hat. "I've heard enough o' this bullshit for one day. We have a job to do, so get serious!"

Thorson had stolen the hat and his black frock coat from a Southerner whose wagon train he and the gang had raided two months ago along the Overland Trail. He was tall, rangy, and black haired, with sharp blue eyes and bushy black sideburns. He would have been handsome if his face hadn't been pitted with buckshot scars, his nose blunt and misshapen from several fractures.

Lips pinched with anger, he again swatted Mahoney with his hat. "I told you boys not to fight amongst yourselves. We're s'posed to be a gang. Remember what happened to Billy Tribble? First one o' you kill's another gang member, I'm gonna cut you up slow for wolf bait."

Mahoney shifted another hard, mocking look at Little Mike, who stared back just as hard but whose hand had stopped its slide to his pistol. Finally, Mahoney gave him a taunting wink and turned his gaze to the valley.

The stage was only a couple hundred yards away now, its clomp and clatter rising on the wind. The driver's muffled yells rose as well, and the long blacksnake cracked like pistol fire.

Pike Thorson checked his pocket watch. Returning the timepiece to his shirt, he said, "Right on time." He leaned back in his saddle and toed his big Appy off the ridge. "Quit your damn bickering and move out. We got work to do!"

As he spurred his paint horse after the leader, Turk Mahoney sidled up to J.D. Brennan.

"Why did Little Mike kill his ma?"

Brennan snickered as he leaned back over his plunging horse's rump, holding the reins chest-high. " 'Cause when he was twelve years old, she got drunk and told him she couldn't believe what an ugly ringtail she had for a son!"

Galloping across the canyon bottom toward the stage road, Brennan and Mahoney threw their heads back and roared.

•   •   •

Inside the rocking, rattling stage, Lou Prophet shifted uncomfortably in his forward-facing seat. Within the tiny confines in which Prophet and six other passengers had been sealed like slugs in a revolver's cylinder, the air hung hot, heavy, dusty, and reeking with sweat.

They were high on the high Wyoming plains, but it was still damn hot, and no one was more aware of it than Prophet, clad in widow's weeds—a woman's high-buttoned black dress with a cape and stitched white collar. The collar pinched his neck until he felt as though the blood had been cut off from his brain. His neck itched so bad he felt like ripping the dress open and hacking at himself with the Arkansas toothpick hanging from a rawhide strap down his back.

Under the pillow strapped to his chest, giving him a bosom the size of a stock trough, sweat ran in rivers down his belly.

The matching black hat with a gauzy black veil didn't help matters. It sealed the heat inside his body, making him feel like a boiling English teapot. The black, square-heeled shoes—the largest he could find—were two sizes too small, which made keeping his feet set primly together beneath the hard plank bench as demanding as keeping mum while rats chewed your privates.

Hoping his wince passed for a priggish smile befitting an elderly widow, he stared out the windows and assuaged his discomfort with remembered images of bathing naked in a clear, flowing creek near his boyhood home in the Appalachians of north Georgia. Interrupting the daydream, an elbow poked his ribs.

He turned to his left and looked down at his partner, Louisa Bonaventure, clad in a summery yellow formfitting dress and looking for all the world like a wholesome young parson's daughter on her way to a church picnic. She smiled up at Prophet sweetly, pushed up on her tiny rump, cupped her hands around her mouth, and whispered in his ear, "Stop squirming, you big idiot!"

She drew away, her feigned smile so bright that her cheeks dimpled, but Prophet recognized the tartness in her hazel-eyed gaze.

He leaned sideways, nudging her shoulder, smiling the old-lady smile he'd practiced so well, and grunted through clenched teeth, "I can't help it!"

Louisa's smile brightened, as though she and Prophet were merely discussing an anticipated pound cake and tea later in Bitter Creek. But as she turned away, Prophet felt the sharp pain of her bony elbow stabbing his ribs.

He turned to the window again, clutching the lumpy, leather reticule in his lap and smiling instead of cursing.

As he did so, he caught a glimpse of the man sitting directly across from him. Since the man had boarded the stage in Rosehawk, he'd either been checking his tarnished silver pocket watch every ten minutes, or making eyes at Louisa. He was staring at her again now, his eyes hooded and leering. Louisa ignored him, staring out the window to her right.

Prophet eyed the man through his veil. He had hardcase written all over him—from his unruly, long blond hair falling down from his shabby bowler to his hatchet face, which he tried to soften with a pair of tiny, green-tinted, rectangular spectacles riding high on a long, broad nose.

He wore a black suit with a fawn-colored vest and polished brogans, but the worn cartridge belt and long-barreled Remington tied low on his right thigh gave the lie to the cheap gambler's duds.

He was no more a gambler than was Prophet a Presbyterian minister.

Prophet shuttled his gaze around the stage, quickly taking in the portly businessman reading a newspaper on the other side of Louisa, and the plain-faced, young woman clad in homespun cotton and holding a blanket-wrapped infant.

The girl's stocky husband, dressed like a farmer, sat between her and the hardcase, directly across from Louisa. The young man snored softly, his chin tipped to his chest, revealing the tattered, sun-faded crown of his black felt hat trimmed with a red squirrel's tail.

Prophet tensed when the hardcase's hand moved suddenly. His muscles relaxed as the man again plucked his tarnished silver watch from his vest pocket, flipped the lid, glanced at the face, and casually returned the old turnip to its pocket.

The man sighed as though bored, leaning forward to look out the window. He gave the passing countryside—a forested ridge beyond a meadow splashed with wildflowers—a casual glance, then sat back in his seat and returned his leering gaze to Louisa, his eyes flickering across the girl's small, firm mounds pushing at the yellow cloth.

Instinctively protective of Louisa while knowing she needed little protection, Prophet felt the urge to kick the man's knee with one of his stout, black shoes, but restrained himself.

As though sensing Prophet's acrimony, the hardcase turned to him. Prophet slid his eyes to the window and tensed, feeling the man's gaze on him, appraising, scrutinizing. Prophet tightened his big, white-gloved paws on the leather reticule, gently squeezing.

The hardcase cleared his throat. "Sure is a lovely . . . uh . . . fine young lady travelin' with you today, ma'am."

Prophet turned to him, prickling with jealous anger. Before he could reply, Louisa gently elbowed his ribs, warning him to keep his emotion on a short leash. Prophet swallowed his anger and considered a feminine response. He'd practiced a high-pitched voice on Louisa before boarding the stage, and they'd both agreed he should open his mouth as little as possible.

Prophet smiled behind his veil and tittered modestly.

"Yessiree," the hardcase drawled, his frankly appraising

gaze glued to Louisa's breasts, "she sure looks like a . . . uh . . . mighty *civilized* young lady."

Politely, her hands folded in her lap, Louisa said, "Why, thank you, sir. I do endeavor to make myself an asset to society."

The man glanced at Prophet, the bridge of his nose wrinkling distastefully. "You two can't be related."

Prophet stared at the man, straining to maintain his mute, witless smile.

"Of course we are," Louisa said. "Aunt Eloise is my dearly departed mother's older sister."

"You don't say. There sure ain't much of a family resemblance." The hardcase tilted his head as he shuttled his gaze back to Louisa. "What do you say Auntie Eloise and I switch places?"

Louisa glanced at Prophet. "Why would you want to do that?" she asked innocently.

The man didn't say anything for a moment. Through a lusty grin, he said, "So we can . . . get better acquainted. Maybe, uh . . . snuggle a little."

Louisa's voice turned hard. "I don't snuggle with strangers, sir!"

The man looked surprised. "You don't? A pretty little piece o' poon-tang like you? What a shame!"

Prophet hoped Louisa would keep a lid on her rage. You never knew what she would do, one moment to the next.

"What did you call me, sir?" Louisa's voice was as sweet as Christmas fudge, but Prophet noted the dangerous edge.

Oh, no. Smiling gently, Prophet placed a hand on the girl's thigh, silently commanding her to ignore the man.

The hardcase's eyes went snaky-flat as they again strayed to Louisa's pert bosom and continued down her slender but well-turned legs sheathed in the form-fitting dress.

To Prophet, he said, "Come on, Auntie. Let's switch places." The man slid forward on his seat.

Prophet's smile tightened into a silent warning. Beside the hardcase, the sleeping young farmer snorted and bobbed his head, chin grazing his chest. The baby fussed, and the farmer's wife rocked the child from side to side. She watched Louisa, Prophet, and the hardcase, a nervous look on her moist, unadorned features. The businessman glanced at the hardcase and quickly buried his face again in his newspaper.

"Come on, Auntie," the hardcase insisted, "let's switch places. You'll get a change of scenery, and I'll . . . well, I'll get acquainted with your lovely niece."

"Aunt Eloise appreciates your concern, sir," Louisa said, and Prophet was happy to hear the equanimity restored to her voice. "But she gets sick when riding backwards. We wouldn't want her getting sick on the stage"—Louisa snickered—"after all the pig's liver and buttermilk she ate at the last way station."

She glanced at Prophet, drawing her full, cherry lips wide with a humorous grin. Prophet turned to her, smiling stiffly.

The hardcase's features blanched and his grin quickly faded. Compressing his lips with defeat, he sat back against the stage's front wall. He said nothing, but his frustrated, lusty eyes played openly over Louisa's body for the next five minutes. Then, as if remembering something, he stiffened and reached for his watch. Before he could open it, guns popped in the distance.

"Oh, my word!" the young mother exclaimed with a start. "What was that?"

"Yes, what was that?" Louisa echoed. She too was staring out the right-side windows, where several horsemen could be seen, galloping across the meadow on an interception course with the stage.

Prophet did his best to look surprised, gasping and

trilling and craning his neck to look out the window with everyone else. Everyone but the hardcase, that is.

A gun hammer clicked. Prophet turned back to the hardcase, who waved his Remington, grinning with smoky delight.

"That, ladies and gentlemen," he said, "is a holdup."

2

"EVERYONE JUST STAY calm and don't try anything funny," the hardcase said, concentrating his attention on the young farmer and the portly businessman, who regarded him fearfully, hands raised.

Sensing the danger, the baby had started wailing.

Outside, the gunfire died as the stage slowed, the driver yelling, "Woooo-oo-ahhhh! Wooooo-ahhhh!"

The Concord rocked and bounced as it slowed, its leather thoroughbraces quacking like ducks. Inside, the blond hardcase, smiling with self-satisfaction, kept his long-barreled Remington aimed at the passengers, making sure no one went for a gun.

Prophet hadn't seen a weapon on either the businessman or the young farmer. If they were heeled, he hoped they had sense enough to keep their iron stowed. Going for guns would only get them ventilated.

The stage stopped so abruptly that Prophet, Louisa, and the businessman had to grab the hanging ceiling straps to keep from being thrown forward. Outside, voices rose above the clatter of prancing horses, commanding the driver and shotgun messenger to throw down their weapons.

Prophet rolled his eyes to the windows while keeping his gloved hands raised.

Four riders appeared around the stage, the blond dust sifting around them. Three aimed pistols. A fourth man—a tall, bull-necked hombre with full red sideburns and crazy eyes—leveled a heavy, double-barreled shotgun at the Concord's right windows.

Gents, Prophet thought with grim satisfaction and a healthy dose of caution, *meet J.D. Brennan of the Thorson-Mahoney Gang.*

Brennan was the gang's newest member, having escaped a federal lockup in Arkansas after strangling three guards and slitting the throat of a fourth with a sharpened chicken bone. The reward for him alone was five hundred dollars—more than enough to give any bounty hunter, including the big-spending, womanizing Prophet—one hell of a shindified night in Denver City . . . if he lived long enough to collect it, that is.

"You hear me, Auntie?" It was the blond hardcase staring at Prophet hard, eyes red-rimmed with rage. "I said, get your fat ass outside, and be damn quick about it!"

Prophet trilled fearfully, clumsily gaining his feet. All the passengers but Louisa had already disembarked.

She took Prophet's hand. In a fear-brittle voice, which Prophet knew to be total playacting—the girl had killed more men than Billy the Kid and would not have blanched at a diamondback under her pillow—she said, "Come, Auntie. Don't be afraid. We'll be all right. I promise we will. . . ."

Prophet stumbled, nearly breaking his ankles in the hard, undersized shoes, and cooed like a frightened crone. As the stage rocked on its thoroughbraces, he accepted Louisa's hand with his left while clutching the lumpy reti-

cule in his right. He took mincing, old-lady steps to the
door.

Finally, the hardcase behind him grumbled, "Oh, for
chrissakes!" and swung his leg up, connecting his polished
brown boot with Prophet's ass. Dress flapping around his
legs like batwings, Prophet flew through the door and hit
the ground on his face.

"Auntie!"

"Oh!" Prophet cried. "Oh! Oh! Oh!"

He lifted his head, spit dirt from his lips, and peered
around. The other passengers stood around him, hands
raised above their heads, faces flushed with fear. All the
outlaws were mounted, forming a semicircle around the
stage. The young mother had left her baby on the stage, apparently believing it safer there, and its hysterical cries rattled eardrums.

"Auntie, are you okay?" Louisa cried, dropping to her
knees beside Prophet, who continued to moan and covertly
study the hardcases.

Glancing at Louisa, he saw that she was doing the same
thing—feigning concern for him while stealing looks at the
owlhoots, getting each one fixed in her mind, waiting for
the right moment for her and Prophet to make their moves.

"Tell that old bitch to shut up!" one of the riders yelled
at Louisa.

"Leave her alone," a chubby, pig-eyed young rider inter-
jected. "She can't help it if she's afraid."

"Good Lord, that's an ugly woman!" another exclaimed.

"Didn't I tell you?"

"Man, I see what you mean."

"Shut up—she can't help it she's ugly."

"Shut up your ownself, Little Mike. If she tried to snitch
a bite off your supper plate, she'd turn ugly in a heartbeat."
The rider slapped his thigh and laughed, pleased with himself.

"All of you, shut the hell up!" the leader said, sitting his big Appaloosa behind the stage driver and the shotgun messenger. Both stage men stood wide-eyed, hands raised high, looking at Prophet expectantly.

The leader jerked his hard, anvil chin around the group. "Mahoney, Brennan, Little Mike—fetch the strongbox and fetch it quick!"

"I can't climb up there," the fat man complained.

"Get your fat ass up there," the leader barked, "or I'll have Brennan carve you a new asshole with his shotgun."

Grumbling, the fat man holstered his six-shooter, climbed awkwardly out of his saddle, hitched his pants up, and tossed his reins to one of the others. He and Mahoney and Brennan headed for the stage.

Prophet had turned onto his ass, keeping his dress down over his legs, his veil over his face. He kept moaning and groaning while Louisa sat beside him, patting his back and assuring him everything would be all right.

Meanwhile, she jerked her head around at the hard-cases, stealing cunning glances at each, waiting. . . .

Horses blew and the baby cried. The stage squawked under the weight of the three men climbing to its roof. The farmer, his wife, and the businessman watched them skeptically.

"This girl here is coming with me," said the blond hard-case with the colored spectacles. He grabbed Louisa's right arm, jerking her to her feet, her straw hat tumbling off her shoulder. "Look at her, boys—ain't she something?"

"Take your hands off me, you maggot!"

The blond hardcase laughed. "And she's got spunk too. Boy, oh, boy, is she gonna be fun under the blankets to-night!" He slapped her hard across the face. Louisa cursed and dropped to her knees, bowing her head, her blond hair falling over her face.

Prophet gritted his teeth with fury, but his voice was appropriately high-pitched and beseeching. "Leave my niece alone. . . . Don't hit her. . . . *Oh, please!*" Behind the veil, his eyes were hard. The blond hardcase was going to pay for that slap in spades.

"Stand up here—let me get a look at you!" the blond hardcase barked, jerking Louisa again to her feet.

Prophet could tell the man's strength was too much for the girl. He wanted to make his move, but checked himself, waiting. If Louisa could hold on until the men trying to free the strongbox on the stage roof had started climbing down, so much the better. . . .

Louisa tried to slug the hardcase, but the man was too fast for her. He grabbed her lashing fist with one hand. With the other, he grabbed the top of her dress and jerked his hand back, ripping the garment off her shoulder, exposing her white chemise and a good portion of her milky cleavage.

Louisa shouted a curse not found in most young ladies' vocabularies—most men's, for that matter. Especially not one with Louisa's angelic face.

Jerking herself free of the man's grasp, she stumbled and fell on her ass between two horses. The startled mounts skittered sideways as their riders laughed and whooped at the girl's exposed flesh.

"Leave me alone, you blowfly!" Louisa screamed, red-faced with genuine anger.

"That's quite a tongue on you, bitch!" the blond hardcase snapped, gritting his teeth.

As he moved toward Louisa, Prophet was about to make his move.

A gun exploded.

Prophet's hands froze, and he jerked his startled gaze at the stage. The three riders were crouched over the strongbox. In Mahoney's hand, a gun smoked. He fired another round at the lock, sparks flying.

"Got it," he said. He opened the lid, glanced inside, and said, "Must be close to ten thousand dollars here!"

"Throw it down," the gang leader commanded. Turning

to the blond hardcase, he said, "Barker, throw the girl over your horse. We don't have time for that now."

Barker cared more about Louisa than the strongbox. Red-faced with fury, he stepped brusquely toward her and dropped to a knee.

"I'm warnin' you—leave me alone, you son of a bitch," she spit through gritted teeth, leaning back on her hands.

"Leave my niece alone!" Prophet wailed.

He glanced at the stage. The three men rolled the strongbox to the edge of the roof and dropped it over the side. It landed with a clanging thud, blowing dust and frightening several horses.

His attention riveted on Louisa, Barker didn't turn.

"I'm warnin' you, you pile of stinking dog shit," Louisa said. "You touch me again, you're gonna be sorry."

"Oh, please leave her alone!" Prophet cried.

"Barker, we don't have time for that!"

Barker sprang forward, grabbed her dress with both hands, and ripped the garment all the way down to her waist. He frowned and stared down at the black gunbelt and pearl-gripped Colt, which looked twice as big as it actually was on her slender hips.

Prophet smiled ruefully, and in his normal voice chided, "She told you to leave her alone. . . ."

Before the sentence had died on his lips, Louisa had clawed the six-shooter from her holster and compressing her lips angrily, thrust the barrel into Barker's gut.

Barker's face blanched instantly as he stared, dumbfounded, at the Colt stabbing his breastbone.

"Die, devil!" She pulled the trigger.

Barker gave a jerk, his spectacles falling down his nose, eyes and mouth springing wide, blood splashing the horse behind him as the slug tore through Barker and into the leg of the rider on his left flank.

As Louisa thrust Barker away from her, she jumped to her feet. Crouching, she commenced firing at the other dumbfounded hardcases, who stared, frozen, their mouths drawn wide.

Prophet waved to the stage passengers and yelled, "Get down! Get down!" as he thrust off his black cape and veil and grabbed the sawed-off double-barreled shotgun hanging from a leather lanyard down his back. Aiming the gun from his waist, he tripped the left trigger and watched the face of one hardcase turn to strawberry jelly.

He slid the barrel toward the gang leader, who was holding the Appaloosa steady with one hand while leveling his rifle. Prophet tripped the shotgun's right trigger. The Appaloosa pitched a half second after Prophet's buckshot tore through the man's chest, and the man twisted and plunged down the Appy's hip with a groan.

Only about three seconds had passed since Louisa had shot Barker.

Above the frightened horses' whinnies and the screams and yells of the passengers, who'd dropped and buried their heads in their hands, Louisa's Colt blazed with purpose—*bang! bang! bang!*—and the hardcases dropping from their pitching, crow-stepping mounts attested to the accuracy of the girl's aim.

Meanwhile, Prophet dropped the barn-blaster. He was reaching for his own Peacemaker strapped to his right leg when he saw Mahoney, kneeling before the stage, level his pistol on him.

As the gun blasted, Prophet threw himself backward. He hit the ground on his shoulder, clawed the Peacemaker off his leg, and twisted around to his belly.

He leveled the Colt and fired. His chest sprouting blood, Mahoney flew backwards against the stage and dropped, wracked with death spasms.

Prophet swung the gun to his left, looking for a target. Seeing little but powder smoke and prone bodies, he turned right.

No target there either.

The baby bawled fiercely from inside the stage. The woman sobbed into her open hands, her shoulders jerking. Her husband, lying facedown beside her, draped his arm across her back protectively.

The driver and shotgun messenger lay nearby. Hearing no more gunfire, both men lifted their sunburned faces warily, glancing around.

Prophet looked at Louisa. She was crouched on one knee, her second pistol—a .38 pocket gun—smoking in her right hand. She too was looking for more targets.

Hearing a yell, Prophet turned to look back the way the stage had come. About a hundred yards away, a horse galloped off into the distance, its rider hanging by a stirrup, hauled across the brush-tufted terrain like a doll dragged by a careless child.

The man's screams died as the horse faded from view.

Slowly, glancing at the hardcases sprawled around him, Prophet climbed to his feet. He frowned, whipping his head this way and that.

"How come I count only five?" he asked Louisa.

"The sixth one's heading that way," Louisa said, glancing after the runaway horse.

"But there were seven."

Seconds stretched.

A man's shout rose above the cries of the baby the woman had left inside, apparently out of harm's way. Prophet's glance jerked to the stage. His right shoulder blade bloody, J.D. Brennan sat in the driver's box, releasing the brake and slapping the reins fiercely over the six-horse team, yelling like Satan on Sunday.

"Hyaaaaaaaaaa! Hyaaaaaaaaaa, team—hyaaaaaaaaaaaaaa!"

The team jumped off its rear hooves and leapt into its halters, digging its hooves into the trail. The stage bolted forward as though propelled from a cannon, the door slapping its frame and popping open again, the baby crying even more fiercely than before.

His feet screaming inside the undersized shoes, Prophet raced for the carriage, dived for the boot, and grabbed the rawhide straps. Behind him, the young mother screamed, *"My baby!"*

As the Concord raced across the meadow, fishtailing on the sandy trail, Prophet clung to the straps, his feet dragging.

Grunting and gritting his teeth with the effort, he reached his left hand up, grabbed the top of the luggage boot, then reached up with his right. He dug both hands into the leather, heaving himself upward until he hooked his right foot onto the boot.

The bouncing carriage beat and pummeled him, and several times he nearly lost his grip and went tumbling onto the trail. His hat and wig had blown off, but the dress whipped against his legs, the collar digging into his neck.

Finally gaining a solid purchase with his right foot, he heaved his body onto the boot. The stage hit a pothole, and he jerked sideways, instinctively reaching up with both hands. Only his left found the brass rail on the carriage roof.

His fingers closed around it as he slid off the boot and dangled down the stage's left rear corner, shoes digging at thin air. The door roared like gunfire each time it hit the frame without latching, setting up a ringing in Prophet's left ear.

Inside, the baby wailed, its voice trembling with the bouncing stage.

Grunting and cursing, twisting and slamming against the carriage, Prophet glanced at the trail passing below in a blur of rocks and grass and short stretches of open sand. The stage hit another pothole, bouncing viciously, and Prophet's left hand slipped.

He cursed, twisted around until he faced the carriage, reached up with his right hand, and closed it around the rail. Cursing and grunting, buttons popping from the dress, the shoulder seams tearing, he chinned himself up over the

Concord's roof until both arms were straight out below him. He swung both black shoes up and threw himself forward against the passengers' trunks and carpetbags.

Heaving a sigh of relief, he lay for a moment, bouncing against the stage roof, staring at the clear blue sky. When he'd caught his breath, he pushed himself to his knees and began crawling toward the driver's box.

He'd moved only two feet when J.D. Brennan swung his head around. Holding the team's ribbons in his right hand, he aimed a six-shooter across his right shoulder with his left hand and fired.

Prophet threw himself left and, doing so, nearly threw himself off the stage. He rolled back to his right as Brennan fired again, but the stage was bouncing too much for the hardcase to get an accurate shot.

Brennan turned back forward when the stage swerved. Prophet slid a carpetbag from under the straps securing it to the stage roof. When Brennan turned back to him, extending the gun and firing again, Prophet threw the carpetbag.

The bag hit the gun, casting the slug wild, then bounced off Brennan's wounded shoulder, off the driver's box, and over the side.

"Son of a whore!" Brennan shouted, wincing with pain as he clutched his shoulder.

He fired again before Prophet could dodge, but the stage bounced at the same time, and the bullet tore into a trunk. Standing with his feet spread, arms thrown out for balance, Prophet crouched, grabbed another bag, and threw it.

As the hardcase turned toward him, the bag hit Brennan full in the face, nearly knocking him out of the driver's box.

As he began turning back and whipping the gun over his shoulder, Prophet dove forward, wrapping one arm around the hardcase's neck and one hand around the gun, shoving it down.

Brennan triggered a shot, which tore into the floor of

the driver's box. The stage careened as the horses spooked, then fishtailed as the team increased its speed.

As the two men wrestled for the gun, the stage swerving this way and that across the trail, Brennan flicked the trigger back until it locked. Twisting right, he thrust the Navy Colt toward Prophet's ribs. At the same time, he slowly maneuvered his finger under Prophet's grip toward the trigger.

Knowing he was about two seconds away from having daylight carved through his middle, Prophet heaved on the gun with all his strength. He felt Brennan's wrist give. The stocky Brennan was tough, but he was sitting too awkwardly to use his strength to his full advantage.

Prophet twisted the man's hand toward Brennan's own ribs.

"Nooooooo!" Brennan raged, watching the barrel snug up against his bloodstained shirt.

Prophet squeezed the man's hand until Brennan's index finger compressed the trigger. The gun barked and jumped. Brennan jerked, stiffened. His eyes glazed as his face blanched. His muscles relaxed.

Jerking the man's gun from his slack hand, Prophet tugged his collar, rolling Brennan's lifeless body off the stage. He watched the hardcase sail down and back, hit the ground, bounce, and roll into the brush along the trail.

Prophet looked around for the reins. Several of the ribbons had dropped from the box and were dragging along the ground, bouncing as hooves stomped them. Several more were lying on the floor of the driver's box.

Prophet picked them up, sat down, planted his old-lady shoes against the foot rest, and sawed back on the ribbons.

"Whoa, horses. Whoa-ahhhhhhhhhhh!"

After the stage disappeared, the passengers gathered in the shade at the edge of the meadow—all but the shotgun messenger, who sat atop the strongbox in the middle of the trail, his shotgun across his knees.

The young mother was inconsolable, howling into her husband's chest while the driver and the businessman, sitting against tree boles, looked on with tongue-tied concern.

"Your baby's just fine," Louisa tried to assure her, casually nibbling a piece of jerky she'd retrieved from her dress pocket. A lone surviving button holding her dress closed, she stood staring up the trail. "J.D. Brennan has five hundred dollars on his head." Louisa chewed and stared in the direction the stage had gone. "Lou won't let him get away."

The mother heard none of it. She cried, "My baby, my baby!" punching her husband's chest with her fists and burying her face in his shirt.

"Shhh, now, Alice . . ."

Ten minutes passed. Finally, the stage driver pushed slowly to his feet, staring east. The stage and horses appeared at the edge of the meadow, moving toward the group at a walk.

"Look!" the jehu yelled, pointing. He laughed.

Louisa watched the stage angle across the meadow, drawn by the plodding, lathered, hang-headed team. Prophet sat high on the front seat, his black dress hanging in tatters down his muscular arms and legs, exposing his faded red balbriggans.

He'd taken off the black shoes and stockings, and his bare, blood-smeared feet were propped on the footrest. His mussed brown hair, touched with gold by the west-angling sun, slid around in the breeze.

In one hand, he held the reins of the lathered team. In his other arm, he cradled the blanket-wrapped baby. Crouched over the child, he made exaggerated goo-goo faces and gurgling sounds, then lowered his head to nuzzle the child's cheek.

"My baby!" the mother wailed, tearing loose from her

husband's arms and dashing across the meadow to the stage.

Behind her, smiling proudly at Prophet, Louisa said, "Told you."

3

A HALF HOUR later, the stage rattled into the little ranching burg of Bitter Creek—an assortment of businesses and ramshackle huts grown up around a stage station and post office in a lonely Wyoming basin.

The carriage churned up dust on the wide main drag and swung to a halt before the stage office sitting between a livery barn and a bathhouse.

The carriage door popped open, and out stepped Lou Prophet, cutting a ludicrous image in the widow's weeds hanging in torn, dusty strips about his six-foot-three-inch bulk. He'd exchanged the pointed, torturous black shoes for his well-worn, undershot boots.

Still, as his feet hit the ground, he winced. The women's shoes had taken their toll, and he wasn't sure his feet would ever be the same again.

"Here we are, folks—the end of the line," he said, holding the door wide.

The young woman with the baby was the first to emerge, still looking wan with relief and holding the child so close to her breast that Prophet worried the kid was going to suffocate.

"I can't tell you how grateful I am," she said, clutching his arm. "You, too, miss," she told Louisa coming out behind her. "Bless you both." She hugged Louisa, then pulled away, once again looking the young, female bounty hunter up and down. "How did you learn to ... do what you do ... *so well* ... ?"

"Practice," Louisa said, characteristically taciturn.

A man's voice lifted to Prophet's right. "Good Lord, what do we have here?"

Turning that way, Prophet saw two middle-aged men standing on the raised boardwalk. The one on the left was balding, clean-shaven, and wearing a green visor and sleeve garters.

The other was several inches taller, bearded, and paunchy. He wore a suit with a five-pointed star pinned to his brown wool vest, but he had the weathered, saddle-seasoned look of a man who'd once ridden the cattle paths, maybe even a few owlhoot trails.

The depot master and the town marshal most likely. They must have been having coffee and doughnuts together. The little depot master had a half-eaten doughnut in one hand, a stone coffee mug in the other. The marshal held a coffee cup as well, and he had crumbs in his beard.

Both men were frowning up at the Concord's roof. Prophet, the driver, and the shotgun guard had tied the dead owlhoots to the roof, wrapped in their own bedrolls. Their horses were tethered to the luggage boot.

The driver had climbed down and was off-loading luggage for the waiting passengers. "That there's the Thorson-Mahoney Gang, Mr. Crumb—all laid out like ducks ready for the stew pot!"

The depot master blinked up at the blanket-wrapped bodies. "The Thorson-Mahoney bunch," he said, glancing at the marshal standing beside him, "is up *there*?"

"They hit us about ten miles outside town," the jehu said, handing the young farmer his carpetbag. "The big hombre there in the widow's weeds and this young lady here filled 'em so full o' holes they wouldn't hold a thimble full of water."

"These two took on the entire *Mahoney* Gang?" the marshal asked, shifting his incredulous gaze from Louisa to Prophet, who held the dress's hem above his boots with one hand as he pulled himself up the side of the stage with the other.

The driver told the depot master and the marshal the whole story, the young farmer and the portly businessman fervently interjecting details. Meanwhile, Prophet produced the Arkansas toothpick from the leather sheath hanging down his back, just below his collar, and began hacking at the ropes tethering the bodies to the brass rails. One by one, he rolled the dead men over the side. They landed with loud thuds, several discharging air upon impact.

The little depot master and the bearded marshal stared, gaping.

As Prophet eased himself into the driver's box, then down to the right front wheel, the marshal stepped down into the street, kicked over one of the bodies, and opened the blanket. He canted his head this way and that and said, "Sure as hell—this is Little Mike Ensor!"

He glanced at the depot master scowling down from the boardwalk, then moved to another body, and kicked it over onto its back. He gasped. *"Pike Thorson!"*

Finished off-loading the luggage, the driver was buckling the flaps over the boot. "They hit us about ten miles out, Marshal. That gent there and the girl kinda rattled their cages a might. Took down the whole damn gang." He grinned big, showing the few coffee-colored teeth remaining in his jaws. "I don't think we'll have any more trouble from these sons o' bitches, unless they come back as ghosts, that is."

The marshal turned to Prophet. His eyes played over the remains of the widow's weeds hanging off Prophet's big frame, as if the dress were part of some joke. "You took down this *whole* bunch?"

Prophet lounged against the stage's off wheel, rolling a cigarette from the makings sack he'd produced from the war bag at his feet. His big, brown fingers worked clumsily, but they were getting the job done. He nodded to indicate Louisa leaning against an awning post atop the raised boardwalk. "Me and her did."

The marshal turned to her and scowled. He looked her up and down. Dressed in her frills, blond, hazel-eyed, and angel-faced, Louisa could have hopped out of some German fairy tale.

"The hell you say!" the marshal grunted.

Prophet grinned and licked the rolling paper.

To the depot master still standing in shock atop the boardwalk, not far from Louisa, Prophet said, "We'd like to collect on the reward, Louisa and me. I think most of the boys only have a couple hundred on 'em, but ole Pike and Brennan each have five. You correct me if I'm wrong."

The depot master glanced from Prophet to the bodies strewn about the stage and back again. "No . . . uh . . . that's right. The express company does indeed have that much on the gang. They've been . . . uh . . . ." He chuckled with dry relief, realizing suddenly that the gang that had been a needle in his side for so long was lying here in bloody heaps in the street. "They've been giving us trouble about every two months for the past two, three years. Preyin' on that strongbox that carries the mine company payroll."

The marshal was moving around the stage, inspecting each body. From the other side of the Concord, he said, "Sure enough, it's the whole damn gang. . . ."

The depot master glanced at Prophet, still vaguely troubled and puzzled. Then he looked Louisa up and down one more time. "Are you trying to tell me this . . . *child* . . . helped you take down the Thorson-Mahoney Gang?" He chuffed. "That I do not believe, sir!"

Prophet regarded Louisa anxiously and muttered, "Uh-oh."

Expressionless, Louisa lifted her cape over the butt of the pearl-gripped Colt jutting up on her right hip. She glanced around briefly, her gaze lighting on the battered tin cup hanging from a nail in the awning post above the rain barrel. In a blur of motion, she crouched and clawed leather.

The Colt roared, ripping the cup from the nail and tossing it into the street.

The Colt spoke again.

The cup bounced ten feet in the air. As it started down, the Colt barked a third time, throwing the cup even higher.

At the apex of the cup's climb, Louisa pinked it once more, blowing it out and away from the stage station and onto the stoop of an abandoned shanty across the street.

The stage team had already been led off to the corral, but the two dogs that had been sniffing around the dead owlhoots ran howling off behind the bathhouse.

Louisa straightened from her crouch. She twirled the smoking gun on her finger and dropped it neatly in its holster.

"Show-off," Prophet said.

The depot master regarded the girl slack-jawed. He glanced at the marshal, who shrugged, then turned to the grinning driver. "Well, if you'll sign the affidavit, Ham, I reckon I'll get started on the paperwork."

With that, he turned and strode into the station.

Prophet started after the man. Behind him, the marshal said, "What's your name, son?"

Prophet turned. The marshal approached him, stepping

around the stage's lowered tongue, his brows furrowed with wary appraisal.

"Lou Prophet," he said, throwing up both hands palms out. "Better not get too close, Marshal. I'm a bounty hunter, if'n you couldn't tell from the death stench."

"I could tell. I don't set much store by your ilk, but the fact is there ain't enough badge-toters to go around. If it weren't for bounty men, the West would be overrun with jaspers like these." He nodded to indicate the dead Thorson-Mahoney Gang. His forehead lined with incredulity, he asked, "The girl hunt bounties too?"

Prophet turned a glance at the raised boardwalk, but Louisa was no longer there. He looked around, frowning. She was nowhere in sight. It was just like her to slip off when there was paperwork to do. Nothing bored her more.

"She does," Prophet told the marshal. "Louisa got started when her family was murdered—butchered, more like—over in Nebraska. Me and her work together on occasion."

"How'd you know this stage was gonna get hit?"

"Didn't."

Prophet took another deep drag on his quirley and noted several curious locals gathering to appraise his and Louisa's handiwork around the stage. "But we knew the gang was workin' this area, and they were due for a strike. We been ridin' the line between Denver and Cheyenne, and Denver and Lyons, and come up dry." He shrugged. "Decided to give this dogleg in the line a shot."

"Why the . . . uh . . . getup?" the marshal inquired, flicking a hand out to indicate Prophet's tattered dress.

"We heard Thorson was putting a gang member on the stages he struck, before he struck 'em, to make the passengers all nice and agreeable." The bounty hunter shrugged, flushing and wanting nothing more than to climb out of the dress and into a hot bath.

The marshal fingered his beard, nodding slowly. "You were afraid you might be recognized?"

"You got it." Prophet smiled affably. He usually resented being interrogated by local lawmen. Understandably, most resented him for doing their jobs for a lot more money, and they used their authority to complicate his life. But this badge-toter seemed harmlessly curious.

No more questions seemed forthcoming, however, so Prophet said, "Well, if you'll excuse me, Marshal. I reckon I probably have some forms to fill out. . . ."

Hefting his war bag, Prophet mounted the steps, wincing against the pain in his forever-pinched feet, and ambled into the station house.

When, twenty minutes later, he'd penciled out a report, and the depot master, Mr. Crumb, had wired his bounty claim to the stage company headquarters in Denver City, Prophet walked back outside, letting the screen door slam behind him.

"Hey, there he is," a man on the street shouted. "There's the bounty hunter that blew the gang's lights out!"

Prophet stopped on the boardwalk, casting his beleaguered gaze into the street. The Concord had disappeared. In its place, a crowd had gathered—twenty or thirty townsfolk with children, babies, and dogs.

Having hunted men for nearly ten years, Prophet wasn't surprised to see the dead owlhoots all laid out, shoulder to shoulder, to get their pictures taken by a man in a shabby checked suit.

The crowd had formed a wedge around the festivities, and several station hostlers hunkered around the dead owlhoots, mugging for the camera. The pistols held dramatically across their chests looked as though they hadn't been fired since Gettysburg.

"Sir!" the photographer called, throwing up an arm. "Would you like to pose with your quarry?"

The hostlers turned their heads to regard Prophet, crestfallen. They didn't want the bounty hunter pissing on their fire.

"Nah," Prophet said. "These boys'll make a better tin-type than I would."

Brightening, the hostlers turned to face the camera.

Prophet donned his hat, hefted his war bag, and turned toward the bathhouse. He was crossing the weedy lot where two mutts were growling over a racoon carcass when a voice sounded behind him.

"Mr. Prophet?"

The bounty hunter stopped and turned. The marshal ambled out of the crowd gathered around the photographer's subjects and approached Prophet with a slight limp.

"What's the matter, Marshal? Don't you want your picture taken?"

"I don't have no use for that stuff," the bearded man said with a dismissive wave. "I have a job for you."

Prophet's forehead lined. "I gotta job."

"Bounty hunting ain't gonna get you far—even with that sharp-shootin' blonde backin' your play." The lawman hooked his thumbs in his pistol belt, canted his head, and frowned with scrutiny. "Tell me, son, how old are you?"

Prophet shrugged. "Thirty-three, thirty-four. Don't know for sure. Ma and Pa Prophet had so damn many kids in them Georgia hills, they couldn't keep track of birthdays."

"Thirty-three, thirty-four's old for bounty hunters. Come to work for me as my night deputy. I already got a kid workin' nights, but I've caught him sleepin' on the job. I'll demote him to weekends."

"I told you, Marshal, I—"

The lawman shook his head. "Not so fast, son. Don't be hasty. This here ain't exactly a civilized town, but I'm makin' some headway with the owlhoots. With the help of a big, capable man like yourself, it could be a nice place to settle down in a few years." He paused, glancing eastward along the street. "You and that blonde, uh, *close*?"

"We're business associates," Prophet said, as if it were any of the marshal's business.

The marshal winked wolfishly. "We got some damn nice-lookin' gals in this here basin. There's a young lady that runs a café. A little large, but she sure can cook, and I have a feelin' cookin' ain't all she does well." The lawman winked and grinned with only one side of his mouth.

Prophet opened his mouth to speak, but the lawman cut in again. "Fifty a month and found," he offered. "Now, it probably don't look as good as that reward money you rake in, but then you have to get awful tired of trail food. Not to mention the prospect of gettin' drygulched every time you round a bend, or gettin' your throat cut after wrappin' up in your soogan at night."

Prophet waited to make sure the man was through. "You see, Marshal—"

"Whitman."

"You see, Marshal Whitman, I made a pact with the devil a few years back, just after I mustered outta the War for Southern Liberty. I told Ole Scratch that if he showed me a real good time here atop the sod for the rest of my days, I'd shovel all the coal he wanted down below. Now, ridin' down owlhoots for two-fifty, five hundred, sometimes even a thousand dollars a head, for two, three weeks work, gives me plenty of lucre for my real good times. And believe me, Marshal, after what I seen durin' the war, I've learned to have *real* good times!"

Whitman opened his mouth to speak, but Prophet cut him off. "And those times are expensive, Marshal. Fifty dollars a month is a right generous offer—especially for a town the size of Bitter Creek. It could even get me through a single night's celebration . . . but what would I do after that?"

Whitman stared at Prophet, lips pursed. He shuffled his polished boots and cursed. Finally, he nodded. "I reckon I see your point. And I reckon I ain't been totally square with you, Mr. Prophet. Fact is, this is a dangerous town. We're very remote, but lots of folks pass through here on their way farther west. Bad folks."

"You're in prime owlhoot country—I'll give you that, Marshal. I'd like to give you a hand, but like I said . . ."

Whitman waved him off. "No. It wouldn't be right—bringin' an outsider into the kind of bailiwick we have here. It ain't just the drifters that's settin' off firecrackers beneath my saddle blanket."

Prophet canted his head, studying the man, who looked off as if seeing his own dark destiny in the wheel ruts along Main. "Bailiwick?"

Whitman turned to Prophet and blinked, obviously distracted . . . worried. "Never mind. Thanks anyway, Mr. Prophet. I hope you have a good time before you drift."

Suddenly, the man smiled his wolfish smile and tugged on his beard. "You might want to take a look at Miss Schwartzenberger over to Gertrude's café, though. She's—"

This time it was a pistol shot that interrupted the sentence. The report was followed by a scream.

The marshal whipped his gaze toward a saloon up the street, before which a half-dozen horses stood tethered to the hitch rack. A man's laugh cut the air.

Whitman's face creased with disgust. "Ah, shit!"

"What is it, Marshal?" Prophet asked, following the lawman's gaze.

The pistol spoke again, causing the horses before the hitch rack to start and pull at their reins. The girl screamed again.

Whitman shook his head angrily and began walking toward the saloon. "Just one of them firecrackers goin' off under my saddle blanket," the marshal said with a taut sigh. As he angled across the street, Prophet saw that while the man had grown paunchy on town food, his shoulders were still wide, the arms thick, his gait certain despite a slight hitch in his right knee. The marshal unholstered his six-shooter and flipped it butt-forward in his hand.

"Need any help?" Prophet called behind him.

The marshal threw an arm out dismissively, mounted the opposite boardwalk, and limped toward the saloon, swinging the six-shooter like a club.

Prophet stared after the man for a moment, then shrugged and turned into the bathhouse.

4

MARSHAL WHITMAN OPENED his eyes with a start, his breath catching in his throat. He lay on the cot in the empty jail cell, staring at the low timbered ceiling, listening.

Satisfied he'd only dreamt the clomp of horse hooves and sudden blasts of gunfire, he lifted his head to peer through the open cell door into the main office. His deputy, Eddie Phipps, sat at the desk that Whitman had hammered together from the bed of an old Texas seed wagon.

A single bull's-eye lantern glowed dimly. The deputy leaned back in the swivel chair, arms folded across his chest, boots propped on the desktop. His hatless, carrot-topped head drooped toward his chest.

"Eddie, goddamnit!" Whitman yelled, his voice caroming off the chinked log walls. *"Wake up!"*

The deputy bolted upright, reaching for the old Remington on his hip while dropping his booted feet to the floor with a crash and several squawks from the swivel chair. Eddie froze, hand on the holstered revolver butt, looking around as though the room were on fire.

"What is it, Marshal? Is it them? Is it them?"

"No, it's not them, you idjit. You went to sleep!"

High-pitched, mocking laughter rose from the cell beside Whitman's.

"Is it them? Is it them?" the voice mocked before breaking into more laughter.

"Shut up, Scanlon," the marshal barked. "If I want any shit out of you, I'll squeeze your head!"

In the shadows of the next cell, Rick Scanlon lay on his cot, one elbow propped beneath his head, casually dragging on a quirley and blowing smoke at the ceiling.

He cackled mockingly. "If I didn't know better, Marshal, I'd say your deputy was a mite off his feed this evenin'. But then again, who wouldn't be feelin' jittery . . . the night they was gonna die?"

Ignoring the young roughneck, Whitman dropped his feet to the floor with a weary grunt and rose. Cursing under his breath, he spit into the sandbox, stretched his suspenders up over his shoulders and sagging belly, and limped into the main room.

"Get up," he told the young deputy.

"Sorry, Marshal," Eddie said. "I was just gonna close my eyes for twenty seconds. . . ."

"Twenty seconds, uh?" Whitman grumbled. "Why in the hell you so damn sleepy? You're s'posed to *sleep* during the *day*. I hired you to work the damn *night* shift."

"Haven't been able to sleep too good during the day," Eddie said. "Reckon it takes a while to get oriented differ'nt."

Whitman reached for his gunbelt, which was coiled over the hat tree behind the front door, and wrapped it around his waist. He canted his head at the cell he'd just vacated. "Go lay down. If you're sleepy, for chrissakes, go to sleep."

"I thought you wanted me to keep watch."

Whitman barked, "But you ain't keepin' watch. You're sleepin'. I'm awake now anyhow. Go lay down. I'll wake you if I need you."

"Hee-hee," Scanlon chuckled within the wavering shadows of his cell. "Hey, what's that?" he said dramatically. "Did I hear my pa comin' to my rescue?" He laughed again.

"And you shut up in there, or I'll take a horsewhip to you," Whitman yelled, poking an angry finger at the cell door.

As the deputy slouched into the empty cell, removing his jacket and gunbelt, the young hardcase said, "Ah, come on, Marshal. What're you holding me for anyway? So I got a little frisky over at the Mother Lode. It's been a tough week."

"A little frisky, eh?" Whitman said, removing his six-shooter from his holster and checking the loads. "You call ordering your men to tie the whores into chairs so you can shoot apples off their heads 'a little frisky'?"

Scanlon said, "It was all in good fun, Marshal."

"I don't think the whores saw it that way."

"That's the trouble with the whores in this dump," Scanlon said. "They ain't only ugly, they got no sense of humor."

"Well, you better hope Mr. Crumb has a sense of humor. He runs a pretty tight ship—you know that."

"I ain't gonna be in here long enough for ole Crumb to play his judge-and-jury games, old man," Scanlon scoffed. All the humor had leeched from his voice. "I'm gonna be outta here in an hour, maybe two. And you and your deputy there are gonna be swingin' from that cottonwood down by the creek."

His voice remained hard, but Scanlon raised it a notch for the frightened deputy's benefit. "Just a-swingin' and a-kickin' and a-tryin' to suck air through your windpipes. Only no air's gonna come, 'cause—"

"I told you to sew it, Scanlon!" Whitman shouted, turning toward the dark cell in which the hardcase lay smoking.

Scanlon chuckled softly.

"Don't listen to him, Eddie," Whitman said. "We're the law in this town. His old man respects that. Deep down he does."

There was a slight pause before Eddie said, "I ain't worried, Marshal."

Scanlon hooted softly.

Whitman glanced into the cell block furtively, then stole out from behind his desk, quietly sprang the front window shade to the left of the door, and peered into the night-shrouded street. Looking first right, then left, and seeing that all was quiet, he gave a quiet sigh.

No sign of old Sam Scanlon's boys.

The marshal directed his gaze left again. The Mother Lode up the street was closed, the wind shepherding leaves along the street, up the boardwalk, swirling them at the base of the saloon's big, plate-glass window. That's where the trouble had started a few hours ago. Where it always started with Old Man Scanlon's firebrand son.

The trouble was, neither Scanlon nor his son had any respect for the law—at least, not for the law in Bitter Creek. And because they didn't, none of their men did either.

Well, that was about to change, goddamnit. Right here and now . . .

Hearing soft footfalls, Whitman felt his heart leap. Giving a start, he turned his startled gaze up the street to his right. A rider materialized out of the darkness, riding a tall black Thoroughbred. As the horse approached, Whitman's heart lightened. It was only the girl who'd ridden to town with Prophet and the dead Thorson-Mahoney Gang—that girl bounty hunter who looked like butter wouldn't melt in her mouth.

She rode straight-backed, chin jutting tensely. Her hat was tugged low over her forehead. The wind nipped at the brim and at the girl's baggy, brown poncho. Her honey-blond hair bounced on her shoulders, fanning out behind her in a wind gust.

The high-stepping Thoroughbred's hooves clomped in the street, barely audible below the wind keening in the jailhouse's chimney pipe.

Where in the hell was she going this time of the night, Whitman wondered, turning his head to follow the girl past the jailhouse and down the street. Leaves funneled between the blacksmith shop and the ladies' millinery, churning into the street behind the horse.

And then the horse and the girl turned the corner around the Methodist church and disappeared. . . .

Whitman stood wondering after the girl, unconsciously grateful for the distraction. Where would she be riding on a cold, windy night? Hell, it was a good sixty miles to—

"Any sign of my old man yet, Marshal?"

Whitman jumped, startled, his heart leaping violently. Bunching his face with anger, he turned to the darkened cell. "Boy, you're gonna get a horsewhippin' if you don't keep that trapdoor shut!"

Scanlon's self-satisfied chuckles sounded softly from the shadows. Whitman ground his teeth together and resisted the urge to poke his Colt through that closed cell door and commence firing. A few years ago, when he was young and a tad wild himself, he might have done just that. If he did it now, however, he knew the outlaws in this woolly country would declare open season on him.

Whitman stoked the old potbelly stove and put coffee on to boil. When the water was bubbling, his night-shift deputy was snoring softly. Scanlon was too, thank Christ.

Whitman retrieved the coffee can from the cupboard above his desk and dumped a fistful into the water. He was about to add one more when a sound rose from the street beyond the front door.

Whitman froze, his fistful of coffee poised above the bubbling pot. The thuds of shod hooves sounded again. Saddle leather squawked—several sets.

Whitman opened his hand to let the coffee fall into the

percolator, then hurried to the window. Peering out, he felt his back draw taut and his chest grow heavy.

Six or so riders trotted in from the right, materializing like ghosts from the darkness. The half-dozen silhouettes pulled to a halt in the middle of the street, directly before the jailhouse.

In the middle and slightly forward of the group sat Big Sam Scanlon—a tall, bulky figure wearing a wide-brimmed black hat. His gray mustaches curled out from both sides of his mouth, bone-white against his shadowed face. He wore a fox-fur coat buttoned up to his throat. His mountain-bred mustang skitter-stepped beneath him, but settled when Big Sam drew the reins taut.

The butt of a Spencer rifle jutted up from beneath Sam's left thigh, within easy reach.

Regarding the jailhouse sternly, Big Sam barked, "Whitman!"

The marshal's heart turned a somersault. He wheeled to the gun rack, calling, "Eddie!"

The deputy came instantly awake, his feet thudding to the floor. His voice owned a nervous trill. "Is it them, Marshal?"

"It's them," Whitman said, grabbing his double-barreled Greener from the rack and breaking it open. "Get your ass up here."

From the locked cell, young Scanlon's mocking cry lifted on a laugh. "Is that my pa, Marshal? Told ye he was comin'!"

Ignoring the hardcase, Whitman turned to Eddie, who was pulling his gunbelt on. "You stay here. Grab a Winchester and whatever you do, don't let those bastards in the building. You been practicing your shooting in that ravine, haven't you?"

"You bet, Marshal," Eddie said, trying to steel his voice as he grabbed a carbine from the wall rack.

Standing at his cell door, lacing his fingers together

around the bars, young Scanlon cackled like a witch. "Ah, come on, Marshal. Why don't you just let me go? You ain't got no help but that kid, and Crumb's cowering under his bed."

"Sew it, Scanlon!"

"You don't wanna die tonight. You don't wanna get little Eddie's neck stretched tonight. . . ."

"Don't listen to him, Eddie," Whitman said. "We're the law here. People gotta respect that or we're no better'n the brush wolves."

"I hear you, Marshal," Eddie said. "He don't scare me a bit. He keeps up his talkin', I'm liable to shove this carbine down his throat."

"Now you're talkin'," Scanlon said with a laugh.

"Whitman!" Big Sam Scanlon called again, louder this time.

A horse chuffed. The rancher's men were talking quietly amongst themselves.

When Whitman had shoved wads down both barrels of his Greener, he braced Eddie with a look and opened the door. Holding the Greener out before him, the marshal stepped onto the boardwalk, then drew the door closed behind him.

"What is it, Scanlon?" the marshal asked, as if he had no idea why the belligerent rancher had come calling so late in the night.

"I hear you been messin' with my boy again, Whitman," Big Sam said in his deep, even voice. He sat his mustang casually, one gloved hand atop the other on the saddle horn.

"I haven't been messin' with your son. He's been messin' with the girls over at the Mother Lode. I told him what was gonna happen next time he got out of line and discharged his firearm within the town limits. He's locked up, and he's gonna stay there till the circuit judge comes and hears his story."

Big Sam stared down at the marshal. The cowboys on either side of him stared as well, their prominently displayed pistols in easy reach.

Big Sam had been an outlaw before he'd come to Bitter Creek and bought a ranch with stolen loot. Most of his men were gun wolves with whom Sam had ridden the long coulees. He used the wolves to keep the miners and grangers from tearing up his graze and squatting on his water holes.

Whitman couldn't see the gun wolves' faces under their hat brims, but he could tell by the set of their shoulders that they weren't smiling.

Big Sam's voice rumbled up from deep in his chest. "You know I don't recognize Henry Crumb's so-called law. Let my boy go, Whitman."

"I can't do that, Sam."

"*Mr.* Scanlon," corrected the tall, loose-limbed cowboy sitting to Big Sam's right.

Holding the Greener across his chest, Whitman glared back at him in silence.

"You let him go," Big Sam warned, "or I'll stretch your neck. No one fucks with me, Marshal. No one. Not you, not Henry Crumb, and not Dean Lovell. It's time you and all these rock-pickers and plow boys got it straight."

Whitman's chest felt heavy and constricted. He took a deep breath, calming his nerves, and measured his words carefully, trying to keep the trill from his voice. "I know you were one of the first settlers in this basin, Mist . . . Sam . . . but that don't make you and your boy above the law. When young Rick comes to town, he obeys Mr. Crumb's laws or I turn the key on him, just like I'd turn it on anyone else. No exceptions. I've given him enough chances to straighten up and fly right. Now it's time he sees Mr. Crumb. He'll probably only get a fine and maybe some probation—"

"One of Crumb's famous fines, eh?" Snarling, Scanlon

rose in his saddle and leaned forward over his horse's long neck and said tightly, "Let him out, Whitman."

By the weak lamplight in the window behind him, Whitman saw the old man's lips bunched beneath his mustache.

"Now!" Sam roared.

"It's not gonna happen, Scanlon. Now, you boys go on home. No doubt Rick'll be along in a few days."

Neither the old man nor the others said anything. The man to Scanlon's right, whom Whitman now recognized as Leo Barnes, Sam's ramrod, turned to the old man expectantly. Scanlon fairly reeked of animosity. Whitman clutched the shotgun before him, his heart thumping so hard he felt dizzy. His throat was dry. Perspiration streaked his bearded cheeks.

He was encouraged by the old man's lack of action. Scanlon didn't really want trouble with Henry Crumb and Dean Lovell.

Feeling that he needed only to press a tad harder to turn Scanlon's bunch for home, Whitman stepped off the boardwalk into the street and thumbed the Greener's right hammer back.

"Ride on home, Scanlon. Don't dig Rick's hole any deeper than he already dug it himself."

Silence.

Only the sound of the leaves swirling along the boardwalks and pelting the dark storefronts. The horses blew and stomped. At the other end of town, where the old miners' shacks lined the creek, a dog was barking furiously.

Finally, Scanlon turned to Barnes. Whitman saw the man's hard face split with a grin. Barnes laughed, and then the others laughed too, as if at an unexpected joke.

When they'd all had a good laugh, Scanlon turned his gaze to the marshal's left. "Okay, Joe!" he yelled with a trace of humor remaining in his voice.

It could have been a trick to divert the marshal's attention. With the hair pricking along his spine, he stepped back, frowning, and turned his head just enough to see the dark corner of the jailhouse behind him. It was blotted out by a figure bolting toward him. Before Scanlon could turn around to face the man, something hard slammed into the back of his head, catching him just above his neck.

As he went down with a groan, his finger tripped the Greener's right trigger. The gun roared as Whitman dropped to his knees, lights flashing in his head and a thousand horses screaming in his ears.

He dropped the shotgun and rolled in the dirt, losing consciousness fast. Vaguely, as if in a dream, he heard Eddie yell. The yell was followed by several shots, each more muffled than the last, until a dark sea washed over the marshal, snuffing the world like a blown candle.

5

LOUISA LAY NAKED on the rumpled, twisted sheets. Smiling seductively, she lay on her side, her head resting on the heel of her right hand, her long, slender legs curled together, delicate feet resting one atop the other.

Her full, smooth, pink-tipped breasts tipped down toward the bed, tantalizingly screened by her left arm. Her hair was a lovely, flaxen mess.

Prophet quickly undressed, leaned down, moved her arm out of the way, and gently suckled her right nipple until the girl was cooing and sighing and scrubbing his head with her hands and clutching at him with her legs.

After his bath, he'd looked all over town for her. Finally, he'd eaten a tough steak at a deserted little café called Gertrude's Good Food, then stomped off to find a room at the only hotel in town, The Cottonwood. That's when the spidery old man at the front desk—it was actually a broken-down kitchen table with a penny notebook for a register—informed Prophet that "his sister" had already purchased a room for them both.

The old man's eyes twinkled knowingly as Prophet, dressed in his trail clothes and hefting his war bag, shotgun, and rifle, thanked the oldster, headed up the creaky stairs to the second floor, and slouched to the end of the hall.

"Louisa, why do we have to go through this brother-sister nonsense every time we check into a hotel?" he asked after their coupling.

Yawning and stretching her arms above her head, she turned to him with her customary impudence. "We wouldn't want the gentleman downstairs to think we were doing anything improper, would we?"

Prophet chuckled wryly and hooked a lock of hair from her cheek with his finger. "You've killed upwards of thirty men, and you're worried someone's gonna think you're doing something depraved?"

"Killing human dung beetles is one thing, sharing a man's room is another." She turned, buried her face in his chest, and wrapped her arms around his waist. "People wouldn't understand how it is with you and me." She rubbed her cheek against his chest. "I love you, Lou."

Prophet ran a hand through her hair. "I love you, Louisa."

"If we love we each other, why are we never together more than a few days at a time?"

With slow thoughtfulness, he said, "Oh, I reckon it's 'cause we each have some oats to sow before we settle down."

She didn't say anything for a time, just held him, enjoying the warmth of his big, muscular body, the slow thud of his heart in his broad chest.

"It's because we both have men to hunt," she said.

"Pshaw," Prophet said. "I don't have men to hunt—just a livin' to make, and it just so happens I make it hunting men. You, on the other hand . . . you . . ." He shook his head again and sighed. "You got the world to save."

Prophet felt her cheek form a smile against his chest. "I'm savin' it too . . . slow but sure."

He held her away from him. She looked up at him, a faint smile quirking the corners of her mouth. "Louisa, you can kill twenty more men. Make that thirty. Hell, you can kill a hundred." He shook his head. "It's not gonna bring your family back."

She flinched as though he'd slapped her. "I've told you before, I don't want to talk about my family."

"Louisa, you're a damn good bounty hunter, but I want you to quit. I want you to cash in your chips and call it a game before someone cashes them in for you."

The smile on her cherubic face blossomed. "Are you worried about me?"

"Yes."

She lifted her face to him, as though basking in the sun of his concern. Finally, she said, "I can handle myself. You saw that water cup."

He chuffed. "I saw, but that kinda display's gonna make you a target. It's gonna get you killed one of these days, Louisa." He stared at her, pleading. "Won't you hang 'em up for old Lou?"

Her smile turned into a frown. "What would I do? Where would I go?"

"Back to Nebraska."

"No one's there." Squeezing her eyes closed suddenly, as though overcome by a sudden pain, she shook her head. "No!" She lifted her chin, wrapped her arms around his neck, and pressed her breasts against his chest. "I don't want to talk about this . . . just . . . just make love to me, Lou."

She brought her lips to his, kissing him hungrily. Not much time had passed since their first coupling, but she clung to him with such desperation that he succumbed to her and to his own reigniting desire.

Prophet had many weaknesses, Louisa not least among

them. Her compact, full-breasted body pushed against him. He held her tightly, kissing her, enjoying her smooth, moist lips against his, her honey-apple mouth opening, her tongue exploring. In a few minutes, they lay entangled on the sagging, brass-framed bed, the springs complaining with the regularity of a speeding metronome.

Later in the night, he woke with a start and turned to her, curled beside him, her face buried against his ribs. She moaned and sobbed, shaking her head and scissoring her legs.

"Louisa," he said, gently shaking her.

She sobbed again, shook her head, her tangled hair sliding across her face. "No . . . please, no . . . !"

"Louisa, it's all right."

Her voice was small, pinched, pleading. "Oh, God . . . *Please don't kill them . . . !*"

He turned onto his side, took her shoulders in his hands, and shook her once, forcefully. He raised his voice. "Louisa, wake up. You're dreaming."

Her eyes snapped open, filled with black horror.

"Louisa, it's all right," he whispered. "It's me. Lou. You're safe." He smoothed her hair back from her face, kissed her flushed, moist cheek reassuringly.

Slowly, the fear left her eyes, replaced with a relieved recognition. She blinked. Her features softened, and her muscles relaxed. She rested her face against his ribs.

Just when he thought she'd fallen back asleep, her shoulders jerked. She sobbed. And then she was crying, an all-out storm of emotion. All he could do was hold her, rock her gently as she was forced by the nightmare to peer down that dark corridor into the past and watch as her Nebraska farm was raided and her family butchered by the mindless, renegade horde led by Handsome Dave Duvall.

Prophet wished he could erase the images from her mind and set her free, but he'd known her long enough to know that all he could do was hold her. He held her close, rocked her gently, caressing her temple with his face, until the storm had passed and she had once again fallen asleep on his shoulder.

He stared up at the ceiling, Louisa breathing softly against him.

Her family had been killed three years ago. It had been a sudden, thunderous attack by sadistic outlaws. The Red River Gang had been out mostly to rape and to terrorize— what more could they get from attacking poor farm families like Louisa's?—and they'd done a good job of it that day on the little Bonaventure farm on Sand Creek, near Roseville in Nebraska Territory.

Louisa had been out selling eggs to neighbors that morning. When the attack had come, she'd been on her way back home, only a half mile from the farm.

Seeing the smoke of the burning house, hearing the screams and the gunfire, she'd run toward the buildings through the trees and brush along the creek. Seeing the horde of laughing, savage-faced men on horseback, she stopped suddenly. Terror-stricken, she dropped to her knees and hid in the brush.

From there, frozen with shock, she watched as her father and brother were shot down in the yard, her mother and two sisters dragged screaming into the brush west of the house, where they were beaten, raped, and shot before the gang got back on its horses and thundered away.

When Louisa had recovered from the initial shock of the raid, she'd taught herself to shoot and to track, and she'd tracked the Red River Gang into the northern territories, killing it slowly, one man at a time as the opportunities revealed themselves, even appropriating one of its horses, the black Morgan she still rode now. She'd killed a half dozen of the gang when she'd met Prophet in Minnesota, and together they'd stalked and killed the rest.

The gang was dead now, including their leader, Handsome Dave Duvall. Yet for Louisa Bonaventure, whose family was gone, her life ruined, the war against all the other Dave Duvalls and Red River Gangs continued.

Prophet turned to her now, breathing quietly against his shoulder—sweet and lovely, with the innocence of a young Nebraska farm girl. Only, her war continued. It would continue, he realized, until she'd either rid the frontier of evil men or died trying. And Prophet's attempting to stop her was like trying to plug a summer rain in Georgia with a whiskey cork.

Prophet woke early the next morning with achy feet and his chest chafed raw from the cornhusk tits he'd worn in yesterday's summer heat.

He yawned, shoved up on his elbows, and looked to his right. Louisa wasn't there. The wrinkled covers on that side of the bed were pulled up to the pillow, which still bore the mark of her head.

Looking around the tiny room lit wanly by pearl light penetrating the single, drawn shade, he saw that her carpet-bag and rifle were gone as well, which meant she'd probably left town.

Disappointment nipped him.

He'd been hoping she'd stay around long enough for them to have breakfast together, but he wasn't surprised that she hadn't stayed till morning. It wasn't Louisa's way. She knew she'd get her share of the reward money when she and Prophet ran into each other again, and she cottoned to good-byes no more than paperwork.

It had always upset him a little that she could slip away without waking him, for a bounty hunter's longevity correlated directly to the keenness of his senses. Maybe he was just more relaxed when Louisa was around. At least, he hoped that was the case.

He blinked and smacked his lips, swimming up from his slumber. He pushed up on his elbows and glanced around the sparsely furnished room, half-consciously looking for some sign of her amidst the hard-backed chair by the window, the shabby bureau with its tin washbasin and stone pitcher, and his clothes and weapons hanging from hooks along the wall near the door.

Nothing—only her faint smell of talcum and cherries tinged with the scent of pine from too many lonely campfires.

He swung his feet to the floor, planted his elbows on his knees, and lowered his head to his hands. Damn, he thought with a sigh. Why don't I just marry the girl?

But he knew the answer to that. She had far too many demons to whip before settling down with anyone, and maybe he did too. She had to get the faces of her butchered family out of her brain, and he had to travel and drink and fornicate until he quit seeing the faces of his friends and cousins lying beaten and bloody on smoky Southern battlefields. . . .

Those first few hours after he and Louisa had parted were damn lonely, though, he noted as he poured water for a whore's bath in the cracked porcelain bowl.

Damn lonely.

When he'd dressed in his faded denims, buckskin shirt with leather ties, funnel-brimmed Stetson, and blue neckerchief, he stepped into the hall, which smelled of sour runners and stale beer, and turned the key in the lock. He'd leave his possibles, including his shotgun and rifle, in his room until after the stage company had wired his reward money.

He might be here a day or two, waiting for the stage line to cough up the bounty. Prophet was always amazed and frustrated by how quickly express companies offered rewards on owlhoots impeding their business, and how slow they were to pay up when said owlhoots were in custody or wolf bait.

On his way down the stairs, he rolled a cigarette. Passing the spidery gent mopping the lobby floor, he nodded and dug in his denim's pocket for a lucifer.

"Is it true what they said?" the old man asked, eagerly looking up from his work. He was wearing a grimy duck jacket against the morning's high-country chill. The potbelly stove near the desk roared and cracked, smoke seeping around the door. "Did you and your sister stop the Thorson-Mahoney Gang's clock?"

"I reckon you could call it that," Prophet allowed, touching the match flame to the quirley. The story must've made the rounds a few times by now. He hoped his money arrived shortly. There was nothing worse than staying on in a town where everyone knew your occupation. For every five men in awe of your abilities, five others saw you as nothing but trouble, and one or two wanted to cut you down by way of earning reputations of their own.

"That musta been some shootin'." The old man shook his head and snapped his dentures. "You a gunslick?"

"Nope, just a lowly bounty man," Prophet said lazily, his mind's eye on a plate of flapjacks and salt pork.

He was on his way out the door when the geezer said, "I don't normally let bounty hunters stay in my abode. Takes too long to get the death stench from the sheets."

He cackled as Prophet turned to look at him over his shoulder.

"In your case, though, I'll make an exception. Pike Thorson—he sure was a thorn in everyone's side around here. Damn near drove us all out of business more than once!"

Prophet stepped outside and regarded the morning. The toothy ridges showed pink in the north, while the rimrocks in the east were a dusty green before the swollen, salmon orb of the rising sun. Closer to town, the prairie grass rippled over the swells. A couple roosters crowed competitively, and the squawk of a well pump filled the air.

Along the meandering main drag lined with old log shacks and newer, whipsawed stores that still smelled of pine resin, proprietors were sweeping the boardwalks or washing windows or shaking out carpet runners.

One man in a green apron was shoveling horse dung from the street before a small, whitewashed grocery store. He tossed each load into the empty space between his store and the unlabeled shanty beside it—probably a whore-house. The half-dozen pens flanking the house of ill repute were probably cribs. Weeds had grown up around the place, the chinking between the logs of the main cabin was crumbling, and the windows hadn't been washed in several dust storms. It all looked like a bad case of the pony drip to Prophet.

Exhaling smoke, he turned toward the café.

He'd taken only three steps when a shrill scream cut the quiet morning air.

A half second later, he was bolting across the main drag, his six-shooter in hand, heading in the direction from which the sound had come. As he ran around the west side of the jailhouse, he wondered vaguely why the marshal didn't come out of his office. The scream had been loud enough to be heard a good mile into the countryside.

Prophet was halfway down the weedy gap between the jailhouse and a drugstore when the scream sounded again, even more shrill this time. It was a little girl's scream, and it made Prophet's heart thud.

He was thinking some pervert was trying to drag the lit-tle girl into the brush along Bitter Creek, when he turned the corner around the jailhouse and froze dead in his tracks, hot blood rushing to his face as he looked into the branches of a sprawling cottonwood.

Two men hung in the tree, their boots about five feet off the ground—Marshal Whitman and a younger, carrot-topped man. Their necks had been stretched a good six inches beyond their normal lengths, and their tongues protruded from their mouths, purple and swollen to the size of small sunfish.

The sounds of retching rose on Prophet's right.

He turned to see two young girls dressed for school. One of the girls, a wiry blonde about ten years old, was on her hands and knees facing the jailhouse, a couple schoolbooks strewn to her right. Her arms were crossed over her stomach. Her head bobbed as her breakfast leapt from her wide-drawn mouth and into the straggly sage clump before her.

The other girl—apparently the one who'd screamed—stood behind the blonde, facing the opposite direction. She was a year or two younger than the blonde. Clutching two thin schoolbooks and a black slate to her chest, she wore a purple poke bonnet trimmed with white lace. Her thick, brown hair fell to her shoulders, which jerked as she cried, casting her tearful, mesmerized, horrified gaze into the cottonwood towering above the alley.

Prophet walked to the girl, pressed her face against his side, and returned his own beleaguered gaze to the tree.

The tin stars on the dead men's chests glistened dully in the morning sun.

6

THE TWO DEAD lawmen hung from the tree, their glassy, half-open eyes staring dumbly at the scuffed, gouged ground beneath their boots. Their hair fluttered in the breeze.

The deputy had obviously been shot before he was hung; blood the color of ripe chokecherries stained the shoulder of his light-blue shirt. Both men's boots turned slowly, this way and that, the ropes squeaking like leather. Whitman's right boot hung half off his foot, showing how hard he'd kicked before he died.

Running footsteps sounded from east and west along the alley and from the spaces between the buildings. The footsteps grew in volume as more townsfolk, having heard the screams, approached.

A woman running around the rear of the drugstore stopped suddenly and clutched her chest. "Oh, my God! Look what they done!"

"For the love of God . . ." a man moaned on Prophet's right. Wretching sounds followed, and Prophet turned to see the portly, balding man bent over, vomiting.

The crowd grew until three fourths of the town was standing around the tree, gazing up at the grisly spectacle. Prophet glanced around at the ground, tufted and furrowed where the lawmen had been dragged to the tree.

Prints of shod hooves made overlapping pocks. It was hard to tell with all the people here now, but he'd say there had been anywhere from five to ten riders in this alley last night.

Finally, when he saw that the gathered, muttering townsfolk were in too much shock to do much but stand, gawk, and shake their heads, Prophet retrieved a barrel standing in the alley behind the drugstore. He stood it on end beneath the tree and climbed on top of it. With his folding pocket knife, he cut through the ropes. When they saw what he was doing, three men moved forward to help. He lowered the stiffening bodies, one at a time, into their hands, and they grimly gentled the dead lawmen onto the ground.

Prophet jumped down from the barrel and collapsed his pocket knife as he gazed at the crowd. "Anyone have any idea who's responsible for this?"

The crowd fell silent, the people glancing around at each other, their brows ridged with befuddlement. Finally, a lean man with a sharp nose and two-day growth of beard stubble lifted his chin at the back of the crowd, near the jailhouse's rear wall. His eyes were tentative as he swung his wary gaze from Prophet to his fellow townsmen.

"Rick Scanlon's gone from his cell. I just checked."

A collective murmur rose again, louder.

One man barked angrily, *"Sam Scanlon!"*

Prophet had just turned to the man when an urgent, female voice rose behind him. "Let me through, let me through . . . !"

Prophet turned to see the crowd parting for a rather plain-faced young woman in a dark blue gingham dress. She was thin and pale and wore her chestnut hair in a severe bun behind her head. She had the look of a school-teacher, and Prophet would have bet several silver cart-wheels that's exactly what she was.

"Dad? Eddie?" she muttered, her eyes drawn wide, her cheeks ashen. Her lips quivered as she bolted past Prophet and dropped to her knees. *"Oh, my God!"* She knelt staring from one body to the other, her hands making nervous gestures over Whitman's chest.

Prophet looked away. When he looked down again, the girl was running her hands down her father's sallow, bearded cheeks and pleading with him to rise.

"Dad? Dad, please!" she begged. "Get up!"

Finally, one of the women in the crowd—a big, ma-tronly sort with gray-brown hair wound in two neat coils on either side of her head—moved forward and knelt beside the sobbing girl. She placed an arm around the girl's shoulders, but the girl jerked away and lifted her swollen, tear-streaked face to Prophet and the other men standing over the bodies.

Her jaw was tight and her lips curled back from her teeth. Her voice was brittle with anger. "This is Scanlon's work, isn't it?"

No one said anything for several seconds. Then a short, fair man wearing a white apron and sleeve garters said guiltily, "We think so, Miss Fianna. Your pa arrested Rick yesterday in the Mother Lode. He's gone from his cell."

Fianna Whitman stared at the man, her gaze filled with such reproach that the fair man's own face blanched, and he glanced away.

As her gaze swept the others, the crowd recoiled from it as though from a sword. "And what are you men going to do about this?"

Another silence hung heavily as the townsmen shared skeptical, sidelong glances.

Finally, someone cleared his throat. "Uh . . . we'll wire the county sheriff, Miss Fianna. . . ."

She trained her squinting glare on the man, who flinched a little. "A lot of good that'll do," she said. "It'll take Dan Ridgely a week to get his old bones out here from Laramie, and by then Scanlon's trail will be as cold as Dad and poor Eddie." Her voice broke on the last. She dropped her chin and pressed the front of her wrist to her quivering lips.

Prophet figured she was barely over twenty, though her manner was that of an older woman, one who'd been saddled with too much responsibility at a young age. Something told Prophet she had no mother.

Gently, a thin woman in wash-worn homespuns, who'd come over from one of the nearby cabins and shanties, said in a slight British accent, "Come on now, Miss Fianna. These men can't ride after Scanlon, face his gun wolves. Why, they'd be killed! We'd all be widows!"

"Everyone who crosses Scanlon ends up dead," agreed a short, portly man in coveralls and a duck coat, a wad of chew bulging his fat red cheek as he stared somberly down at the bodies.

"Sure would like to see an end to Scanlon's hell-raising, Miss Fianna," another man said. "But, well, you know—"

Prophet's face and ears had been warming for the past several minutes. "Oh, for chrissakes," he finally blurted out, amazed by the townsmen's lack of spine.

He figured he didn't need to introduce himself; in a town this size, everyone knew who he was by now.

He shot a look around the crowd. "Your lawmen have been murdered. Murdered and hung. No citizen with half a teaspoon of sand would stand around while the killers rode free." He stopped and stared at the men, who avoided his passionate gaze. "I'll track the men who did this, but I won't go alone. I'll need at least eight of you to even up the odds."

He paused to study the crestfallen faces around him. "Who's in?"

He looked around the crowd. It took nearly a minute for one hand to raise. It started a slow, short ripple through the crowd, at the end of which Prophet counted eight raised hands.

"All right," the bounty hunter said with a nod. "You meet me out in front of the jailhouse in an hour, with saddled horses and at least two days worth of provisions."

The men who'd raised their hands slinked away from the crowd, looking regretful, the others watching as though the volunteers' names had been called by the Grim Reaper. A couple of women clung to them, sobbing.

The girl knelt over her father, the dead man's hand clasped in both of hers. She gazed up at Prophet through two brown tear puddles, her upper lip quivering.

"Thank you, Mr. Prophet."

"Thank you, Mr. Prophet," the girl had said. The phrase echoed in Prophet's brain as he rode at the head of the eight-man column curling into the foothills of the Laramie Mountains, south of Bitter Creek.

"Thank you, Mr. Prophet," he mimicked now, tipping his hat brim down to keep the sun from his face, glancing back to make sure the faint-hearted townsfolk were still on his trail. "Thank you, hell. Thank you for gettin' yourself killed dusting outlaws you never even heard of, for folks you don't owe a damn thing. And hell, there ain't even any reward involved!"

"What's that, Mr. Prophet?" the man named Wallace Polk said, riding directly behind the horse Prophet had borrowed from the owner of the Bitter Creek Federated Livery Barn and Wagon Rental rent-free, since he was riding on the town's business.

"Uh, I was just sayin' the trail must head into the Laramies."

"I'm not a tracker, but that's how it looks, I reckon."

"Scanlon have a ranch out here?"

"That's what people say, but I've never known anyone who knows where it is. Lawmen have tried to track him before, to no avail."

"To no avail, eh?"

This asshole Scanlon seemed to have everyone in Bitter Creek buffaloed like captive white girls at a Kiowa powwow.

Poor Whitman. Poor Fianna.

"I would have to be around when it happened, though, wouldn't I? Goddamn my luck!"

"What's that again, Mr. Prophet?"

"Uh . . ." The trouble with riding alone so much was that talking to yourself became such a habit that you often didn't even know you were doing it. "I was just sayin' we best stop at the spring yonder, give the horses a blow and a drink."

They stopped for fifteen minutes, climbed back into their saddles, and rode until the sun set behind the western mountains, cloaking the killers' trail. As they rode, Prophet learned from several others that Scanlon did indeed have a ranch somewhere in the Laramie Mountains. No one knew exactly where.

The outlaw leader had once ridden the owlhoot trail in Texas before he and his son, Rick, drove a small herd into Wyoming and made a halfhearted attempt to earn an honest living. It didn't take the Scanlons long to learn they just weren't cut out for the back-breaking labor a profitable stock business required. Before their second Wyoming winter, they'd formed their own owlhoot gang of misfits from Texas and Missouri and started preying on stagecoaches, freight trains, and isolated banks like that in Bitter Creek.

When they weren't breaking the law in obvious ways, they made general nuisances of themselves in Bitter Creek, where Marshal Whitman had been growing too old and weary to do much about it.

After every big job they pulled, they hightailed back to their ranch in the godforsaken Laramies, the compound of which no lawman had ever been able to find.

Dry-camping in a hollow, the posse nibbled jerky for supper and washed it down with tepid springwater.

Prophet wanted no fires, in case the killers were watching their backtrail. To his surprise, the other members of the posse did not complain. In fact, though they'd ridden hard all day and most of the men were Main Street businessmen, unaccustomed to long days in the saddle, there had been little grumbling at all.

Maybe they'd only needed a leader to help them rise to the challenge of running down a gang of cold-blooded killers.

Each posse member took turns keeping watch throughout the night. At the first flush of dawn in the eastern sky, they all rose, ate more jerky with water, tacked up their horses, and continued riding south. They rode silently, with grim determination, with a fearful but purposeful air.

At two o'clock in the afternoon, with a brassy Wyoming sun beating down on the rocky knolls and sandstone buttes, they traced a circuitous route through a long valley, wending through the rabbit brush and wild mahogany. At the head of the column, Prophet halted his sweat-soaked mount abruptly and raised his right hand for the others to do likewise.

"What is it, Mr. Prophet?" asked the mild-faced Polk, who ran the tiny drugstore he called the Health Tonic and Drug Emporium beside the jailhouse. "Time for another break? I sure could use one. My saddle galls are acquiring saddle galls."

"I agree," said Milt Emory, riding beside the druggist. He was a lean man with a high forehead, deep-set eyes, and wearing a threadbare white shirt, suit slacks, and brogans. Long, sweat-soaked hair hung down from his floppy-brimmed black hat. Owner of the Bitter Creek Valley Lumber Company, Emory had put his dull twin sons in charge while he was away, and the worry of it shone in his dark, heavy-browed eyes. "I think my—"

"Shh." Prophet squinted into the distance, across the brows of two hills, onto a bench furry with dusty green scrub. The flash came again, like the reflection off glass or metal, amidst the scrub at the bench's peak.

His heart increased its rhythm, but he kept his voice low and calm as he half-turned in his saddle to regard the others with gravity. "Boys, real nice and easy now, we're headin' into that ravine yonder—ahead and right. Real casual . . . like we're all just headin' for a shady place to smoke."

He gigged his buckskin ahead and quartered the horse right, following a meandering game trail off the rise. The others followed, murmuring curiously.

"Mr. Prophet, what is it?" Polk asked, riding off the tail of the bounty hunter's buckskin.

"I think we're bein' set up nice and sweet for a drygulchin'." As Prophet told Polk about the reflection he'd seen on the bench about two hundred yards ahead, he slipped his Colt from its holster and inserted a fresh shell in the chamber beneath the hammer, which he usually kept empty for safety reasons.

He had a feeling it wouldn't be long before he'd need all six rounds and more. . . .

7

WALLACE POLK LOOKED around, frowning, swinging his incredulous, blue-eyed gaze from left to right. "You mean, you think the Scanlon Gang's nearby?"

"I'd love to think it was some circuit-ridin' sky pilot readin' the *Book of Common Prayer* around a coffee fire with a tin pot makin' those reflections, but we best assume it's the Scanlon boys linin' us up in their rifle sights. If it really is some harmless drifter, I'll be the first to apologize with my hat in my hands, but for the time bein', I want you boys to start a coffee fire of your own, at the bottom of this here ravine."

"What's the point in that?" asked the portly, pie-headed banker, Ralph Carmody, his face red as his black Morgan negotiated the grade, throwing the banker forward in his saddle so that he had to push off the horn to keep from crushing the family jewels. Turning in his own saddle to look behind, Prophet noted the gray, curly-headed man, pushing sixty, had sweated up a good, gray derby.

"You hunt birds, Mr. Carmody?"

"Waterfowl," the banker said in a pinched voice with a nod.

"Well, look at the coffee fire like a bunch of decoys you lay out on a slough of an autumn morn . . . just at the edge of the cattails."

"I see," Milt Emory said, sounding none too happy. "We're gonna sort of call them in . . . to us."

"Now we're talkin' the same lingo," Prophet said as he brought his horse to a halt in the crease between two hills, at the edge of a shallow, narrow gully filled with briars.

As he tied the buckskin to a wild plum bush, he told the others his plan. "Gather some wood and build a fire. Not too big, not too small. Throw some green leaves on it, so it smokes up nice . . . but not too nice. Too much smoke might make those killers suspicious. Just a little, so they'll write us off as tinhorns who don't know any better than to send up smoke signals."

"I'd know better than to do that," Carmody muttered indignantly, picking cockleburs from the deerskin leggings he wore over his fawn trousers.

"When you've got the fire going," Prophet ordered the group, "climb to just below the brow of that hill." He pointed west, to the low, rounded ridge. "Belly down and take your hats off, and for God's sake, don't show your faces over the ridge top. Keep your rifles out of sight too."

"What are you gonna do, Mr. Prophet?" Polk asked, shucking his shiny Winchester from his saddle boot. His mild blue eyes glittered excitedly, like sun-shot marbles.

Prophet dug in his saddlebags until he found his moccasins—a ratty but comfortable old pair for which he'd traded an old Ute war chief a deck of cards showing naked saloon girls. He sat on a grassy hummock, tossed the moccasins down beside him, and began kicking off his boots.

"It's what *we're* gonna do—you, me, and Ronnie," the bounty hunter said. "We're gonna sneak around the north side of this hill, hunker down on that shelf yonder, and see if our decoy attracts any game. If so, the boys here will have them in their rifle sights from the east, and we'll have them from higher ground in the north."

"You ready?" Prophet asked Polk and the young man named Ronnie Williams—a sullen but earnest young man, banker Carmody's grandson—who did odd jobs around town, including stringing chicken wire and digging privy holes.

He had longish, strawberry-blond hair under a brown derby hat, a spade-shaped beard, scraggly mustache, and thin lips that rarely smiled. His old Spencer rifle had seen better days, the cracked stock held together with wire and twine, but the others said Ronnie was the best deer and pronghorn hunter in town. Prophet figured a sharpshooter would come in handy atop the ledge he was heading for.

The kid nodded solemnly, eyes wide.

Polk licked his lips and squeezed his well-oiled Winchester. "Lead the way."

"Don't make any moves until I do," Prophet told the others. "Any questions?"

"Just one thing," Sorley Kitchen said—a wiry man, pushing fifty, dressed in faded denims and a blue-checked shirt, who walked with a pronounced limp.

A former camp cook who'd fallen from his own wagon during a stampede, Kitchen repaired pots and pans and painted houses on occasion, when someone in town could afford paint.

"Could we actually brew coffee over the fire? I sure could go for a cup of joe!" He smacked his lips.

Prophet chuffed. "Sure—why not?" he muttered as he turned and headed north along the base of the western hill.

Somewhere above, in the faultless blue sky, a hawk shrieked. He hoped it wasn't a bad omen. He wanted to nail the killers, but he also wanted to get these tinhorns back to Bitter Creek alive.

And himself.

Prophet led Polk and Ronnie Williams about fifty yards north of the other posse members then west another fifty yards and up a steep rise. It was a moderately hard climb, with the layered, chalky shale giving way beneath their boots so that several times each man slipped and had to grab junipers and sage shrubs for purchase.

Once, young Ronnie grabbed a dwarf chokecherry under which a diamondback was napping. The snake woke and struck, nipping the kid's shirt sleeve before Ronnie jerked his hand back. He slid several feet back down the slope on his butt. But the excitement gave him an adrenaline burst, and ten seconds later he was sitting on the shelf's crest beside Prophet and Polk.

He was breathing hard and he looked flushed, but when Polk asked him if he was all right, he just grinned and gave a nervous chuckle, wiping the sweat from his forehead with the shirt sleeve in which two tiny round holes showed, a half inch from the cuff's bone button.

The three crawled to the southern lip of the shelf and hunkered behind boulders shaped like squashed mushrooms. Prophet peered through a notch in the rock, casting his gaze out and down at the flat, scrub-tufted ground between the hill behind which the rest of the posse lay hidden, and the flat-topped butte where he'd seen the sun flashes.

From behind the low hill to his left, a shaggy mare's tail of smoke rose. Just about the right size, Prophet thought. The kind of fire the members of a tinhorn posse might start if they got a little sloppy about the wood they used for a cookfire.

Prophet looked at the flat directly beneath the shelf.

If there were indeed men on the butte—and he was go-

ing to feel like a fool if there weren't—they'd have to tra-
verse that stretch of sage and rabbit brush to investigate the
smoke wafting from the posse's coffee fire.

If there were indeed men on the butte . . .

After fifteen minutes, he was wondering if the reflections he'd seen had only been that of the afternoon sun off
mica shards or water from a spring. If so, he was wasting
precious time while the killers hightailed deep into the
Laramies.

Gazing through the notch, Prophet was about to spit a
curse through pinched lips when he ducked suddenly and
felt adrenaline spurt in his veins. On the flat, he'd spied
movement behind a frowzy cottonwood stand and a tangled patch of wild plums.

To his right, Polk had seen his reaction. "What is it?"
the druggist asked.

Prophet didn't say anything. Casting another careful
glance through the notch, he again saw movement—a
shoulder and part of a hat moving through the rabbit brush
on the other side of the trees.

"Gentlemen, I think we have a barn dance," Prophet
whispered to Polk and Ronnie, who were lying tensely on
their elbows, holding their rifles with iron grips. "In about
a minute, we should know for sure."

He peered through the notch again, saw three . . .
four . . . five men moving through the brush along the base
of the shelf. The men walked abreast, about ten to fifteen
feet apart. They held rifles across their chests as they traced
serpentine courses through the high desert foliage, staring
straight ahead at the ridge before them and at the shaggy
white smoke billowing and tearing against the sky.

Prophet bit the inside of his cheek and felt the blood
coursing slowly but purposefully through his veins. Too
impatient to wait where they'd been, the owlhoots had
taken the bait.

He turned to Polk and Ronnie. "You boys stay here.

When I start shootin', pick a man out of the group and shoot from the top of these rocks. I'm gonna go down and storm 'em, try to take 'em by surprise."

He looked at the two men sidelong and added wryly, "Just don't shoot me in the back."

Polk gulped and adjusted his derby. "You got it, Mr. Prophet."

Prophet had grabbed his Winchester and risen to his feet. He turned back to Polk. "Folks who call me 'mister' make me nervous."

With that he jumped onto the mushroom-shaped rocks at the edge of the shelf. Quickly scouting the slope below, he scrambled from one rock to another, swiftly making his way down the shelf's gently sloping, rock-strewn wall, keeping his eyes on the men below.

He'd get in as close as he could before cutting loose with the Winchester. . . .

He'd just leapt a low shrub, landing on a flat boulder about halfway down the slope, when one of the men turned and saw him. He was the third man out from the slope, wearing black jeans, black vest, and a wide-brimmed black hat.

"Hey!" he called to the others. Wheeling, he dropped to a knee and raised his rifle to his shoulder.

Before the man could fire, Prophet snapped his own rifle to his shoulder and squeezed the trigger. The whip crack of the rifle echoed off the buttes and hills. The killer's rifle popped as he flew backward off his feet, the slug sailing skyward.

The others had turned to Prophet now. They all fired at once as he leapt onto another rock to his right, crouched, and fired again. The man closest to him whipped his head back with the force of the .44 blow to his temple, did several dancelike pirouettes before tripping over a log.

One of the others cursed loudly and ran back for the cover of the cottonwoods. The others dropped where they'd been when they'd first spotted Prophet and began kicking up a furious fusillade. Their faces bunched with frustration as Prophet avoided their bullets by hopping like an Indian from rock to rock, zigzagging down the mountain, pausing on rocks only to raise the Winchester to his shoulder and trigger shots before leaping onward.

The killers' bullets plunked into the rocks and shrubs around him, twanging and clanging with the ricochets.

Meanwhile, as Prophet hopped and fired, hopped and fired, his fellow posse members from the ridge to his left began triggering their own rifles, as did Polk and Ronnie on the ridge behind and above him. From what he could tell as he skipped around the buzzing bullets and took hasty aim from his shoulder, only Ronnie actually hit any of the outlaws. He put one bullet through a man's right eye, dropping him like a tin can from a fence post.

As the man fell into the arroyo at the base of the cottonwoods, Ronnie gave a victorious whoop, his jubilant cries echoing above the intermittent cracks of the rifle fire.

"Don't get cocky, kid," Prophet muttered as he hurdled a shrub at the base of the slope. He ran twenty yards, leapt over one of the dead killers, saw another owlhoot dart out from behind a stunt pine and run toward a boulder.

Prophet stopped and fired two quick shots from the hip. The killer, a man with red hair hanging to his shoulders and clad in a tattered deer-hide vest and battered hat, dropped to a knee, clutching his left side.

He tried bringing up his big Yellowboy repeater. Guessing he'd fired all the rounds in his Winchester, Prophet took the rifle in his left hand, grabbed his Colt .45, and shot the man through the forehead.

He went over with a groan, dropping the Yellowboy and flopping around on his back for ten seconds before he wound down like a child's toy and died.

Crouching, pistol extended before him, Prophet made several slow circles, looking around for the next onslaught.

No more men ran toward him shooting, however. Several lay dead and bleeding, one hanging over a hawthorn shrub, blood pouring from the bullet wound in his chest and from the many small puncture wounds made by the shrub's stiletto-like thorns.

Someone was groaning and cursing just south of him. He walked that way, threading around the shrubs and cedars, until he saw the man. He was dark-haired, with an unshaven, handsome face, tall and lean, wearing black denims and a white pinstriped shirt and suspenders. He wore two holsters on his hips, positioned for the cross-draw, but only one still held a gun—a pearl-gripped Remington.

Rolling on his back, he clutched his wounded right knee and turned his dimpled chin to Prophet, screaming, "My knee! Oh, Christ, my knee! Jesus, it hurts!"

"I reckon it would," Prophet said, glancing around to see if any more killers lurked nearby.

The brush was quiet. The bounty hunter walked over to the wounded youngster and stared down without mercy. He leaned down, grabbed the Remington from the kid's holster, used its barrel to poke his hat back on his head, and clucked his tongue. "Yeah, I bet that hurts like hell."

Hearing footsteps from both the west and the north, he swept his gaze that way. His fellow posse men were jogging this way, holding their rifles up defensively, gazing around at the killers lying twisted and dead over rocks and shrubs, attracting flies.

"Well, well, well," the banker, Carmody, exclaimed as he approached, glaring down at the knee-shot youngster. "Young Rick sure don't look very dangerous now, does he?"

"I'll say he don't!" the lumberman, Milt Emory, said with a nervous chuckle. "None o' these boys do!"

"Goddamnit!" Rick Scanlon exclaimed through gritted teeth, clutching his bloody knee. "For the love o' Christ—help me!"

"Yeah, we'll help you, all right," Carmody said. "

help you the same way you and your old man helped Marshal Whitman and young Eddie last night." He looked at the other men. "Someone get a rope!"

"No," Prophet said. "There ain't gonna be no hangin'."

Carmody and the others looked incredulous.

"What on earth are you talking about?" the banker exclaimed. "There's absolutely no doubt him and these others played cat's cradle with Whitman and young Eddie's necks! I don't much care about Whitman, but Eddie—"

One of the other posse members coughed loudly, cutting the banker off. Curious, Prophet frowned and turned to the man, who averted his gaze and feigned a yawn. Prophet wondered what Carmody hadn't liked about Whitman, but there was no time to pursue the matter.

Prophet returned his gaze to the banker and shook his head. "No Judge Lynch. That ain't the way I work."

He might have skirted around the edges of the law at times, but there were certain lines he did not cross. In his line of work, the area between good and evil was just too gray. If you didn't want to become as bad as the men you hunted, you had to follow a strict set of rules—including the one that said you never killed except in self-defense. Even when an outlaw was wanted dead or alive, or was as vile as Rick Scanlon.

Carmody chuffed and shook his head while Rick Scanlon begged for help.

"You'll get help when we get back to Bitter Creek," Prophet told the outlaw. "If you don't bleed dry by then."

He knelt down and was about to remove his neckerchief to use as a tourniquet when young Ronnie walked in from the north. "Hey, Mister . . . I mean, Proph—I looked over all these dead men, and I don't see old Sam nowhere."

"Me neither," Polk said, stepping between two cedars as approached from the east. He was breathing hard, ener-
d from the gunplay, as were the others. "You said there

were nine sets of horse tracks, right? Well, there's eight men here, Mr. Prophet, and none of 'em is old Sam."

Prophet straightened and looked around, one hand on the butt of his .45, silently chastising himself. He should have counted the dead men, made sure all nine riders had been accounted for. Such sloppiness was a good way to get yourself greased.

8

"EVERYONE, FAN OUT and keep your eyes peeled," Prophet ordered.

He drew his gun and looked around once more, then knelt beside Rick Scanlon, who was sitting on his butt now and breathing hard, red-faced, through his teeth. "Where's your old man, boy?" Prophet asked him.

"Go diddle yourself!"

Prophet thrust the pistol at the younker's face with his right hand and grabbed the heel of the kid's right foot with the other. He gave the foot a jerk.

The kid screamed and pointed. "Over the hill . . . he stayed there!"

"Why'd he stay there?" Prophet asked, tugging on the foot again, causing more blood to ooze from the wounded knee.

The kid gave another yell. "He didn't think . . . he didn't think you'd be all that trail-savvy."

When the kid had started yelling, several of the other posse men had returned, running to see what was going on. Sorley Kitchen chuckled without mirth and stuck his chest back. "This boy who just gave you some ventilation is Ronnie Williams. I'm Lou Prophet. We're members of the posse that just put your gang in the obituary column—all but your boy, that is. Poor Rick's in a bad way, though. You better come with me."

Behind Prophet, Ronnie chuckled.

Prophet tossed the old outlaw's pistols and knife onto the ground near Ronnie. "Present from Scanlon, kid." Gesturing to indicate the rifle leaning against a nearby tree, he added, "That Sharps over there looks right nice as well."

Ronnie glanced at the weapons. He looked at Prophet, jaw hanging. "C-can I have those, do you think?"

"This old bastard ain't gonna have any more use for 'em. Not where he's goin'."

"Holy shit!" Ronnie said.

As the kid bolted for the Sharps, the old man climbed slowly to his feet, grunting. In spite of his wounded shoulder, he swung sharply toward Prophet, bringing a right-fisted haymaker up from his feet. He yelled like a warlock loosed from hell.

The bullet had slowed him, however; he was more bark than bite. Prophet stepped back, easily avoiding the wounded man's punch. As Scanlon stumbled past Prophet's right shoulder, the bounty hunter jerked the butt of his Winchester up and connected it smartly with the side of the outlaw's head.

Scanlon staggered and fell, clutching his torn ear.

He grunted and cursed, regarding Prophet with fury in his dung-brown eyes. "I'm gonna kill you for that!"

"I wouldn't count on it," Prophet said mildly. Then, with more venom, he said, "You got two horses to saddle—one for you, one for your boy. Best get a move on. You got ten minutes. If they aren't saddled by then, I'm gonna let the kid sight in his new rifle on your knees."

When Scanlon had both horses saddled ten minutes later—a blue roan and a wild-eyed paint—Prophet made him lead both mounts by the reins as the three men headed east around the hill.

Prophet walked to Scanlon's left, the boy slightly behind, admiring his new Sharps but berating Scanlon for letting sand get into the breech and for the scratches on the forestock. Scanlon cursed the kid without turning to face him.

"Pa!" Rick Scanlon cried when Prophet, the elder Scanlon, and Ronnie appeared around a cedar, the two horses walking side by side behind. "Jesus . . . goddamnit, Pa!" young Scanlon wailed. "That son of a bitch put a bullet in my knee!"

Carmody and the other posse men had laid out the seven dead outlaws in a line and were sitting or standing around, smoking cigars and admiring their trophies.

"How'd these two bastards know where to find me so fast?" the elder Scanlon asked his progeny, who now sat with his back to a tree, both legs extended, clutching the bloody knee, which no one had yet bandaged.

The kid scrunched his eyes and stared at his father, befuddled.

"Oh, he told us right off," Prophet said, grabbing the canteen looped over the paint's saddle horn. "As soon as I gave his leg a little tug." He popped the cork and drank.

Scanlon curled his lip and stared at his boy, who stared back at him, fearful, sheepish.

"After all I done fer you?" Scanlon raked out, showing the few stained teeth left in his jaws.

"Ah, come on, Pa," Rick Scanlon beseeched. "They woulda found you. This knee o' mine—goddamn if it don't hurt worse than anything I ever had to endure before in my life!"

"Shut up, you damn sissy!" Sam Scanlon ordered his son. "You want these men to think you're a damn Nancy-boy?"

"Don't look to me like he was worth hanging two lawmen, Sam," Ralph Carmody said snidely. "Why, that's what he is exactly—a damn faggot!"

"All right, all right," Prophet said, stepping between the men. To Carmody and the others he said, "Can you boys help the wounded youngster there onto his horse while I take a piss? We can probably get several miles back to town before sunset, but I ain't goin' anywhere till I empty my bladder."

Prophet had a good stream going on the other side of the horses, when a sudden gunshot cut the air and made the horses leap.

Peacemaker in hand and fumbling his dong back into his pants, Prophet was running around the rear of the horses when another gun barked—this one a big-caliber rifle— and Sam Scanlon stood up straight. The old outlaw stumbled back against a small cottonwood. Prophet saw that he had a pistol in his hand.

Scanlon dropped the pistol as he stood there against the tree for several seconds, shaking and jerking. Then he dropped to his knees and fell forward onto his chest, revealing the fact that the back of his head had been blown out when the rifle slug had exploded inside his skull.

Raking his eyes around the shaggy circle of posse men, Prophet saw Rick Scanlon lying at young Ronnie's feet. He was no longer sighing or cursing from the pain in his knee. The bullet in his forehead, right between his beady eyes, had ended all that.

"H-his old man grabbed Mr. Carmody's gun," Ronnie said defensively, wide-eyed from shock. "He shot Rick. He was gonna shoot me next . . . and then I shot the old man."

Prophet saw smoke curling from the barrel of the Sharps .56, which Ronnie held in his hands. Ronnie looked at the damage the big rifle had done to old Sam's head.

It was mostly just a pile of blood, brain matter, and broken bone. It resembled a shattered clay pot spilling Indian stew. The liver-colored blood glistened as the late-afternoon sun found it.

Ronnie made a choking sound, then turned, dropped to his knees, and vomited. Almost immediately, three or four of the other posse men were voiding their paunches as well.

Carmody held a handkerchief over his mouth as he bent to retrieve his long-barreled Smith & Wesson from Sam's fingers.

Prophet inspected the scene grimly and shook his head. "I reckon y'all won't be up for liver stew tonight."

Prophet suggested he and the other posse members bury the bodies of the Scanlon Gang and throw a few rocks over the graves. But Ralph Carmody and the others insisted they tie the dead men to their horses and trail them all back to Bitter Creek, so that Fianna Whitman could have the satisfaction of seeing the bullet-riddled corpses of the men who'd killed her father.

"I have to agree with Ralph," Polk said. "She and all the other citizens should see with their own eyes that the miserable Scanlon bunch is at last out of commission for good."

"Probably help them all sleep better," someone else suggested.

Prophet knew that the men's reasons for trailing the bodies back to Bitter Creek had as much to do with gloating as with pacifying their fellow citizens, but there wasn't much he could do about it. Hoisting the bloody bodies across their mounts and then tying them down so they wouldn't fall off seemed like a lot of unnecessary work, but hell, if they wanted to do it, so be it. Maybe they were right—maybe the law-abiding people of Bitter Creek did deserve to see what had happened to their lawmen's killers.

More importantly, maybe the spectacle would set an example for others with similar inclinations.

It took a good hour to gather all the horses and bodies and get the posse mounted and on the trail again. It was a slow-moving procession, with Prophet leading the posse back north along the canyon toward the tableland.

The stiffening dead men lay over their saddles, their horses tied tail to tail. The kid, Ronnie, held the reins of the lead horse in his right hand as he rode drag, trailing his grim cargo of dead men tied to the saddles of horses made jittery by the blood smells.

They'd ridden barely an hour and a half before the sun slipped beneath the purple western ridges, and the shadows tumbled down from the canyon's rocky peaks, cooling the air. Swifts and swallows hunted, their wings flashing like small-caliber pistols along the canyon's rim.

Prophet saw several small herds of mule deer foraging along the tawny hillocks at the base of the canyon's gradually rising walls.

"Keep moving," he told Polk and Carmody riding behind him. "I'll catch up to you in a few minutes."

"Where you going?" Polk asked.

Prophet shucked his Winchester from the boot beneath his thigh and gigged his horse toward the hillocks rising in the east. "To get supper," he said, and spurred the buckskin into a lope.

Ten minutes later, the posse men heard a shot. Fifteen minutes after that, hoofbeats sounded behind them. Turning in their saddles, they saw Prophet approach in the gloaming, a small muley buck flopping behind his saddle.

He trotted past the long line of riders, dead and alive. Taking the lead again, he lead them into a cove in the hills bisected by a shallow stream and flanked with cottonwoods and willows.

Prophet found a charred fire ring between the stream

and the trees and a few prints, but he didn't think the camp had been used in several days, and then only by passing drovers.

It would be as good a place as any to bivouac for the night.

It wasn't long before the dead men were laid out on the gravel along the stream and the horses were picketed on a long line strung through the trees. The other men built a fire while Prophet skinned and quartered the deer, and then they had all four quarters roasting on spits made from green willow branches.

As the night deepened and the men ate, there was a festive quality as the day's events were recounted in amazed tones. They were all tired, however—"dead-dog tired," as Carmody put it—and not long after they ate, most rolled up in their soogans near the fire and sent up deep, rumbling snores toward the stars that hung like Christmas trimmings in the tops of the cottonwoods.

9

PROPHET KEPT WATCH from two A.M. to three, slept for a few hours, and rolled out of his dew-damp soogan just after the birds began chirping and the dawn made a milky smudge behind the eastern rimrocks.

He made enough noise starting a fire and setting coffee to boil that the others gradually woke, grumbling against their tight muscles, sore bones, and sun-blistered faces and necks. They rose, stomped into their boots, rolled and tied their blankets, and leathered up their horses.

After a quick breakfast of left-over venison and coffee, the group, including the dead Scanlon Gang—a little stiffer, more bloated and blood-crusted—was mounted and riding north through grass that dampened the horses' hocks and glittered like diamonds as the sun rose.

To Prophet, it was just another day in the saddle, and he wasn't all that eager to return to town. In fact, if he'd had his own horse and his reward money, he'd have lit a shuck. The others, however, unaccustomed to having their asses chafed by saddle leather and roughing it under the stars, were eager for stiff drinks, hot baths, and soft beds.

No one said much until the mountains and foothills receded behind them and the roofs and smoke-billowing chimney pipes of Bitter Creek rose out of the ruffling prairie grass and wind-blown sage ahead.

"EEEEEE-*howwwwwwwwww*!" exclaimed young Ronnie Williams, holding his "new" Spencer rifle over his head as he spurred his horse into a lunging gallop over the last rise toward town. The horses sporting the Scanlon Gang galloped along behind, the dead men's heads and legs bobbing stiffly on both sides of their saddles.

The others perked up then too and gigged their horses into trots or lopes. Prophet held his own buckskin to a walk, however, riding easily in the saddle, his funneled hat brim shading his face. He just couldn't get his blood up over a town, especially a town he was long past ready to leave. A nice little box canyon somewhere in the Bitterroots sounded better to him about now—complete with a waterfall and good grass for old Mean and Ugly, fresh antelope or prairie chicken, and a bottle of Arkansas applejack in his saddlebags.

"Come on, Mr. Prophet," yelled Wallace Polk over his shoulder as he rode away. "We have some celebrating to do!"

He'd celebrate, all right—in a dark saloon corner with a bottle of rye. Then he'd head over to the telegraph office and see if his money had been wired. If so, he'd buy himself a bath, a meal, and a tall bottle of Bitter Creek's best rye.

He threaded his way through the shanties and log cabins along the outskirts of the village, then turned onto the main drag.

While the posse whooped and hollered out in front of the mercantile, calling for all the saloon customers and businessmen and ladies to come out and see the cats they'd dragged in, Prophet rode over to the mercantile.

He turned his buckskin over to the swamper. Then, his shotgun slung over his shoulder and his Winchester in his

right hand, he walked back to the Mother Lode, hoping to
kind of edge around the crowd and sneak through the
batwings without being seen by the other posse boys.

He wasn't in the mood for a celebration. Killing even
horned devils like the Scanlon bunch left him sour, and he
was glad it did. When it didn't, it'd be time to retire his
Greener and maybe start repairing tinware or shoeing
horses for a living.

"Someone get the photographer!" someone called,
while the others busied themselves with cutting the ropes
holding the dead Scanlon Gang to their saddles.

The saloon was vacant, everyone including the apron
apparently having gone out to see the dead men. Prophet
helped himself to a beer. He tossed his last nickel onto the
mahogany and took a seat at a table near the back of the
room. He leaned back in his chair, sipped his beer, and
looked out the saloon's dusty window at the crowd gathering around the posse on the mercantile's wide loading
dock.

The town's photographer, in his cheap suit and bowler,
stepped into the street puffing a cheap cigar. He began setting up his camera, struggling to separate the wooden legs
and get them seated in the wheel ruts.

Meanwhile, Polk, Carmody, and the other posse men
were laying out the dead Scanlon bunch in the street, on
planks propped against the mercantile's loading dock. The
posse men were talking like Romans at a lion social, while
the onlookers and listeners exclaimed and shook their
heads with interest.

Prophet sipped his beer and smiled.

Let them have their fun. After all, the Scanlons were a
sizable gang out of their hair. One big pain in the ass, gone.
Maybe now the town could hire a marshal and a new
deputy and get back to normal.

Prophet ran a thumbnail through the beard stubbling his
jaw, remembering his curious conversation with Whitman

the day before he'd died. The lawman had alluded to dark trouble in Bitter Creek. Could he have meant the Scanlon Gang . . . or something even darker?

Prophet shook away the thought and sipped his beer. Whatever the marshal had meant, it was of no concern to Prophet. He kicked a chair out and was propping both feet on it when young Ronnie Williams, Wallace Polk, and Ralph Carmody crossed the street to the saloon. Carmody rose up on the toes of his dusty, black shoes and stuck his pie-shaped, sunburned face over the batwings, squinting into the shadows at the back of the room.

"Ah, I thought we'd find you here, Mr. Prophet." The banker jerked his head, a beckoning gesture. "Come on out and get your picture taken with the Scanlons!"

"You boys go ahead."

"Nonsense, Mr. Prophet," objected Polk, who pushed past Carmody and shoved through the doors. He crossed the saloon, weaving through the tables upon which a few half-empty beer and whiskey glasses sat. Ronnie and Carmody followed, all three making a beeline for Prophet's table.

"Boys, I don't like gettin' my picture taken," Prophet objected, grimacing as the others surrounded him. "It's kinda like the Injuns see it—I'm afraid that box'll take my soul. And since the devil already has it . . ."

"Oh, don't be a spoilsport, Lou!" young Ronnie cried, tugging on Prophet's right arm while Polk tugged on the left.

"All right, all right . . ."

Prophet didn't have the energy or the heart to resist. He knew these men wanted their own pictures taken for posterity but would have felt foolish if he—the man who'd taken down most of the gang—didn't get his taken too. Wearily and feeling embarrassed about the whole thing, the bounty hunter got up and allowed himself to be led across the floor, through the doors, and onto the street.

He was jerked through the crowd and up the steps to the loading dock. The rest of the posse was already hunkered down on their haunches, above the dead gang members propped on the boards.

The posse men all had their pistols and rifles out, held across their knees or over their chests as they stared steely-eyed at the box camera set up in the street, though the photographer hadn't even gone under the curtain yet.

"Oh, for chrissakes," Prophet muttered.

A few seconds later, he found himself hunkered down, in the middle of the group, half the posse on one side, half on the other. Ronnie knelt beside him, holding the Sharps between his knees. Ralph Carmody crouched behind the group, his head just behind and above Prophet's. He wasn't holding his six-shooter, but he'd folded his coat back to display it prominently on his right hip.

"Get your gun out, Proph," Ronnie said.

Prophet was staring at the camera like it was about to fire minie balls. "What?"

"Swing your barn-blaster around to the front, so the camera sees it. You gotta look tough."

"That's all right, kid," Prophet said, smiling woodenly as he faced the box. "You look tough enough for both of us."

The photographer waved all the kids and dogs away from the shot, then ducked behind the camera while the crowd, standing in two wedges on either side of him, watched.

Prophet saw an attractive young lady in a black bodice and see-through wrapper eyeing him admiringly. It made him feel self-conscious, but also heavy down in his loins. It also made him raise his chin a little higher and gather a little steel in his gaze as he stared hard at the camera.

"All right, steady now, boys . . . steady . . ." the photographer admonished from under the black wool curtain. "Steady now . . . steady . . ." Prophet stared so hard his eyes watered. He blinked at the same time the camera popped and flashed. And then all the posse members stood, several clapping him on the back and leading him back down to the street.

"Come on, Proph, the drinks are on us!" Carmody insisted. "A thing like this—wipin' out the whole Scanlon Gang only a few days after blowing the Thorson-Mahoney bunch back to hell where they came from—why, that's cause for celebration indeed. And believe you me, mister, you won't be buyin' one solitary drink tonight!"

Prophet couldn't argue with that. He was out of money, at least until he could get over to the telegraph office. He'd seen the depot master in the crowd, looking pleased as punch at the dead Scanlons, but he hadn't found the opportunity to inquire about the reward bounty. He'd have a few drinks with the boys, then head that way. . . .

He and the others were stepping through the batwings when the good-looking girl Prophet had seen in the crowd stepped up to him. The crowd stopped for her, as did Prophet.

She was a short but long-waisted blonde with blue and green feathers in her hair and with a shape that would have stopped a cavvy of galloping broncs in mid-stride. Powder-white breasts spilled out of her black bodice like twin scoops of ice cream, mercifully drawing the eye from her rather heavy-handed face paint.

Her head barely rising to his chest, she looked up at him wistfully. "So you're the gent that took down the Scanlons?"

Prophet's ears warmed. He shrugged and was glad to have Ralph Carmody answer for him. "He certainly was, Miss Janice. This is the famous bounty hunter, Lou Prophet, who's taken down not only one but two gangs in only a few days!"

"Proph here has saved this town from ruin!" Wallace Polk exclaimed, clapping Prophet on the shoulder.

"Well, in that case, mister," Janice said, canting her head and shutting one eye to stare up at the big bounty hunter wistfully, "you deserve an extra special treat on the house." She smiled at the others. "Don't you think, boys?"

All agreed with hearty laughter, slapping Prophet on the back as the girl led him toward the room's rear by his right hand. His ears and cheeks were as hot as a locomotive's boiler, but he didn't object. Getting his ashes hauled was going to be a hell of a lot more fun than getting his picture taken.

She led him up the stairs at the back of the saloon's main hall. Prophet admired the sexy hitch in her git-along, nearly salivating at the prospect of taking the girl's round butt in both his admiring hands. When she'd opened one of the doors on the left side of the hall, she led him inside, shut the door, and turned to him, smiling alluringly.

"You have no idea how happy I am to have the Scanlons dead," she said, her voice growing hard and her eyes snapping a bit but the smile remaining. "As if we didn't have enough trouble without them adding more. . . ."

There it was again—another allusion to trouble. It went in one of Prophet's ears and out the other as he watched her remove the wrapper, drop it, and begin unlacing the corset.

"Well . . . I was glad to oblige," Prophet said, watching heavy-throated as the girl's smooth, pale hands loosened the whalebone's ties.

The corset bobbed away as her breasts sprang free. The garment dropped and two full breasts lay before him—porcelain-white and pink-tipped. They were the most delicate of fruit, highlighted by the window behind her and slightly to the left.

When she reached up and back to loosen the bun at the back of her head, the smooth, pale globes drew up and flattened against her chest. Her hair fell down across her shoulders, and the breasts resumed their natural shape once more, alluringly framed by the rich blond hair that owned a touch of sunset red.

The girl's full red lips spread with a smoky smile as she moved toward him, rose up on her tiptoes to kiss him. He fondled her breasts gently, and she leaned back with a swoon. Slowly, she began unbuckling his belt and unbuttoning his fly. When the trousers and his summer underwear fell below his knees, her eyebrows arched.

"Oh . . . my . . . !"

Prophet grinned. "You do know how to start a man's fire."

"Yes," she said breathily, gently stroking him, inching her face slowly toward the object of her attention. "Yes, I reckon I do."

Then she closed her mouth over him and, as he eased toward the bed, she went to work showing him—in the kind of expert fashion he'd known only in cities like Denver and St. Louis and once in the lodge of an Indian chief's talented daughter—how pleased she was that he'd snuffed the Scanlons' candles and sent them all to hell with coal shovels.

10

"YOU SURE ARE a well-built man, Lou Prophet," Janice cooed as she tattooed his broad chest and tight, rope-muscled belly with kisses, long after they'd gotten on a first-name basis.

Naked, he lay back on the sheets, which he could tell by the starchy smell and crisp feel had been washed only that morning, and stared dreamily up at the lemon rectangles the west-angling sun made on the hammered-tin ceiling. Absently, he squeezed the girl's left breast with his right hand and sighed with contentment.

"Thank you, Janice. You ain't built so almighty bad your ownself." He frowned at her. "I been in the saloon a few times and didn't see you. Where do you keep yourself anyway?"

She planted a soft kiss on his belly button, then rose up onto her knees. She straddled him, her pale orbs, mottled now from his whiskers, swaying this way and that. In her right hand she held a water glass half-filled with whiskey she and Prophet had been sharing.

"The gent who owns the place, Burt Carr, doesn't think I should work the main room with the other two girls. He thinks stayin' upstairs and only comin' down for special occasions or to sing on Saturday nights gives me an air of mystery."

With that last, she sipped the whiskey and threw her head back with theatrical drama, tittering. Then she gave the glass to Prophet and massaged his equipment back to life with her own.

"I see," Prophet said. The girl gently engulfed him in her warm, moist center. A deep, happy fog streamed over him with the golden sunlight angling through the window. "But I don't think a girl of your, uh, talents needs any such smoke and mirrors to make her more enticing. You do just fine your ownself."

She tittered again. "Why, thank you, Lou. You're gonna give me a big head!"

"Wouldn't be nothin' you ain't already done for me," he chuckled, his chest shivering, ". . . four times, by my last count. . . ."

Before he and Janice were through, the other posse men began yelling up at him, telling him to quit lazing around all day and to get down there and help them celebrate the demise of the Scanlon Gang. Prophet and Janice ignored them, though they got louder and louder. Someone even banged the ceiling with a broomstick or something.

"Oh, I guess we shouldn't be rude," Janice allowed, taking Prophet's wide, scarred, sun-seared face in her hands and planting a brusque peck on his nose. "But God, I could stay here all week!"

Prophet reckoned she was right, and after they'd each taken a sponge bath and helped each other dress, Prophet and Janice left the room and headed for the stairs. They strolled arm-in-arm down the staircase at the rear of the main hall and joined the crowd that had grown so large several men had to stand in the open batwings to drink their beers.

Prophet hadn't walked far before a beer was thrust into one hand, a whiskey shot in the other. He got separated from Janice for a while, and then she was on his knee as he sat at a table in the middle of the room, surrounded by townsmen standing or sitting, all drinking beer or whiskey or tequila and generally stomping with their tails up.

After a few drinks, the world got hazy. It kept getting hazier until he was only vaguely aware of being helped up a staircase that kept skittering out from under him like the deck of a storm-battered ship. The world became a dark, warm arena of vague, erotic sensations punctuated with the sounds of girls cooing, sighing, and tittering.

Then it went black altogether.

He didn't know how much time had passed before he awoke. Opening his eyes and blinking against intense, golden light sending razorlike javelins careening through his brain, he found himself lying facedown on a soft bed, one foot on the floor as if to keep the world from spinning.

He blinked again, lifted his head, and turned from the light. Two girls lay beside him, one practically on top of the other, one wedged so tightly against him their skin stuck as if glued. He saw that, under the fan of blond hair in her face, the one closest to him was Janice. The other was a sandy-blonde, shorter and plumper than Janice, lying facedown, her head on Janice's right shoulder, facing the opposite direction.

Tracy, her name was. Or was it Stacey? Possibly Lacey . . .

All that Prophet could remember about the girl was that she had one blue eye, one brown eye, and a bawdy laugh. He also had some vague, half-remembered images of Janice and Tracy getting nearly as friendly with each other as they had with him.

Prophet groaned and put the brunt of his weight on his left foot clamped tight against the floor. Janice stirred and muttered sleepily, "Mornin', Marshal."

Prophet frowned down at her as he pushed himself to a sitting position, planting both feet on the floor.

Marshal?

She must have had as much to drink last night as he, and was imagining she'd spent the night with Whitman. Hard to imagine Prophet being mistaken for the older Whitman, though.

And a little insulting . . .

He stood and was pleased to note the room no longer spun, but only wobbled a little. He and the girls had slept without covers, but the room owned a morning chill in spite of the sun slanting through the windows, so he covered them both with a quilt. As he did so, Janice yawned luxuriously, stretched her arms over her head, catlike, then turned onto her side, muttering, "Oh . . . I feel so safe. . . ."

Prophet grunted, chuckling, and reached for his underwear. Pulling on the threadbare underclothes, he smacked his lips, noting the taste of whiskey as well as beer and tequila. It made his stomach roll, tempering his desire for a cigarette.

When he had his jeans on, he reached for the buckskin shirt lying over a chair back. Something clattered against the chair. Something solid and tinny.

He held up the shirt with one hand and scowled. He blinked again, only vaguely aware of the ball-peen hammers smacking both temples in unison. Pulling the shirt closer to his face, he studied it as if some dog had shit on it.

But that wasn't a dog stain up there over the right pocket sewn with cow gut. It was a five-pointed star on which the words BITTER CREEK MARSHAL had been engraved.

Suddenly, he was as sober as a Baptist sky pilot. "What the hell is this all about?"

He turned to the two sleeping beauties in his bed, elongated lumps under the rose-trimmed white quilt. "What the hell is this all about?" He held out the shirt in his right fist.

Tracy sighed and rolled over. Janice moved her right foot and mumbled into her pillow, "Not now, Lou, please. We really need our sleep." And then she was again breathing deeply through parted lips.

With mute exasperation, Prophet plucked the star from the shirt, jammed it into his jeans pocket, and quickly donned the shirt. No longer trying to be quiet and ignoring his throbbing, hungover brain, he stomped into his boots, grabbed his gunbelt off a bedpost, and wrapped it around his waist.

Looking around, he saw with relief that someone had brought his rifle and shotgun up from downstairs. Grabbing both, he stalked out of the room, closing the door behind him and donning his hat.

"Mornin', Marshal," greeted the barman, sweeping up last night's liquor- and tobacco-stained sawdust at the bottom of the stairs. The tall balding man smiled up at Prophet ingratiatingly. "Did you have a good time last night?"

"I must have had such a good, heel-stompin' ole time that someone pinned this here badge on my chest." Prophet dug the star out of his shirt pocket and flipped it in his hand. "You don't know nothin' about that, do you?" He couldn't remember the man's name, if he'd been told.

The man stopped sweeping and held the broom's handle in both his callous-gnarled hands. "Why, sure. Don't you remember? Henry Crumb—that's our mayor and the depot agent—talked ye into takin' the marshal's job . . . at least until your reward money for the Thorson-Mahoney bunch gets wired to the bank anyways. We sure do appreciate that, Mr. Proph—I mean, Marshal!"

The barman grinned, showing big, chipped, tobacco-stained teeth and red-rimmed eyes. No doubt, he'd joined in last night's celebration.

"Crumb, eh?" Prophet grumbled thoughtfully, giving

the star another flip. "Much obliged—uh, what was your name again?"

"Burt Carr's my handle, Marshal. I hope my girls pleased you well enough. Anytime you want another roll in the proverbial hay—"

Prophet kicked an empty bottle and headed for the saloon's front doors, his pulse throbbing angrily.

Outside, he got his bearings and headed for the telegraph office, nearly getting run down by a battered yellow farm wagon in the process.

"Sorry about that, Marshal!" yelled the grizzled old-timer on the driver's seat, yanking back on the reins of his beefy dun.

Prophet snarled and continued across the street, mounting the opposite boardwalk.

He was frowning at the shades drawn over the stage station's two front windows and at the placard tacked to the door: OUT OF TOWN ON BUSINESS UNTIL NEXT TUESDAY.

"Next *Tuesday*?"

An unseen projectile sliced the air about two inches in front of his nose and shattered the window behind him. He heard the rifle's crack a half second later as, recoiling from the bullet's close passage, he stumbled sideways. Tripping on his own feet, he hit the boardwalk.

He cursed and jerked a look across the street. A rifle barrel flashed sunlight as a gunman ducked behind the false facade jutting above the bank's shake roof.

Leaving his shotgun on the depot's boardwalk, Prophet grabbed his fallen rifle, sprinted across the street, and ran along the east side of the bank. He bolted around the bank's rear corner and dropped to a knee, snapping his rifle to his shoulder and gazing into the alley over the rifle's front sight.

Shipping crates lay scattered along the building's rear wall. Hearing hoofbeats to his left, Prophet jerked his gaze that way in time to see the blur of a horse and rider galloping around a log shack, heading south.

Prophet straightened and looked around quickly.

Down the alley behind him, a saddled gray mare was tethered to an iron wagon wheel. Prophet ran to the horse, quickly untied it, leapt into the saddle, and spurred it hard down the alley, turning south around a stable, angling around the shack, and looking around. His heart thudded with rage as he urged the horse southwest.

Fifty yards ahead, the gunman dropped below a ridge. Prophet took the ridge at a gallop. At the crest, he peered down the other side to see the man galloping into a draw sheathed in scattered cottonwoods, heading southwest.

Prophet spurred the horse and bent low over the gelding's neck, urging the horse down the ridge, then reining it into the draw. The horse was heavy and old, not made for speed, and Prophet cursed as he caught brief glimpses of the fleeing gunman through the trees and brush littering the shallow cut.

The man was steadily outdistancing him.

Prophet gritted his teeth as he stared around the lumbering gray's lowered head. "Get back here, you cowardly son of a bitch!"

Nothing he hated worse than a bushwhacker.

His adopted horse didn't have much speed, but it did have bottom, he discovered. Slowly but resolutely, he and the gray followed the gunman's trail into a low jog of hills about three miles southwest of Bitter Creek. Prophet knew the odds of catching the man were against him, but there was a slim chance the man's horse was built more for speed than distance. That meant, if Prophet kept after him, he might eventually catch up to him.

He had little doubt about what he'd do then. First, he'd find out why the man had tried to perforate his hide, then he'd kill him. On the frontier, bushwhackers were never allowed to bushwhack again.

That thought was foremost in his mind as he followed a coulee along the base of a high, grassy bench. When he saw where the bushwhacker had suddenly left the coulee and climbed the bench, Prophet ducked and reined the horse sharply left. It was an instinctive dodge in case the man, having climbed to higher ground, had stopped to place Prophet in his sights again.

He had.

The sound of the shot rang out just after the bullet had sizzled over Prophet's right shoulder, where his neck had been only a half second before.

The old horse whinnied and lunged forward. Prophet rolled out of the saddle, hit the ground on his shoulder, and rolled back right along the base of the rise. Startled by the first shot and then by a second bullet tearing up sod to Prophet's left, the horse lunged forward, nickering and loping away.

Taking his Winchester in both hands, Prophet jacked a shell in the chamber and slid a look up the grassy, sage-tufted rise. A granite spine rose from the bench's peak. To the left of the spine, smoke puffed.

Prophet jerked his head down as the slug tore into the slope a foot above, blowing up a sage tuft and rolling it across his shoulders.

"Bastard," Prophet raked out.

He jerked upright, extended the rifle, and fired. His bullet ricocheted off the rocks at the bench's peak with a shrill whine. He rolled back off his left hip and crawled back along the base of the slope. When he'd crawled ten yards, he rose again and squeezed off two more rounds at the spot from which the shooter had fired.

His chances of hitting the gunman were slim, but he thought he could possibly pin him down behind the rocks, then sneak around the base of the slope, possibly flanking the son of a bitch.

Ducking low, Prophet waited for return fire. Nothing.

High above the hill's crest, a hawk screeched. Along the slope a gopher chittered angrily.

Keeping his head low, Prophet crawled back along the slope's base for about fifty yards, rocks and shrubs clawing at his shirt cuffs and denims. Turning left, he ran up the slope, crouching behind rocks and shrubs to glance at the rocky spine looming over him. The slope was steep and his lungs were raw, his thighs screaming by the time he crested out and walked slowly toward the spot from which the gunman had shot at him.

The man was gone, leaving boot prints in the thin layer of sand and gravel around the rocks and a wind-twisted cedar. Prophet hunkered down to inspect the oval print where the man had knelt on one knee, no doubt propping his rifle's barrel on the rocks before him.

Prophet looked around, seeing no sign of the gunman along the slope tapering in the northwest to a deep draw thick with brambles. Beyond were more hills and brushy draws. Prophet scowled and cursed. Impossible to track the man through that. Even if he could, he'd have to find his own horse first, and by then the shooter would be miles away.

Who was the bastard? Why had he been so determined to bed Prophet down with snakes?

A half hour later, Prophet was wandering the prairie on the south side of the bench, looking for the gray horse. On a knoll to his right, a horse whinnied.

He wheeled and raised the Winchester toward the rifle-wielding rider silhouetted against the western sky.

11

"PROPH, THAT YOU?"

The voice belonged to Ronnie Williams. Prophet lowered the rifle slightly. The kid gigged his horse down the hill. When the hill instead of the sky was behind him, Prophet saw the kid's shabby hat, his pale face with the anemic beard, long hair blowing out behind him in the wind.

Ronnie held a rifle across his saddle bows. The chest and withers of his chestnut gelding were lather-foamed, as though the horse had been ridden hard.

"What's all the shootin' about?" Ronnie asked.

Prophet regarded the kid suspiciously. The kid was known to be a good marksman, and several of those slugs had come close to hitting their target.

"How long you been out here, boy?"

The kid's blue eyes flickered. He shrugged. "I reckon I got out here about dawn. I'm huntin' deer for Miss Frieda over to the café. Her special tomorrow is deer stew." He glanced around. "Where's your horse?"

Prophet's glance fell on the .56-caliber Sharps set

across the bows of Ronnie's saddle while he kept his own Winchester raised, held in both hands across his chest. Ronnie lacked a killer's rough edges and cunning eyes. In fact, he was the last person in Bitter Creek whom Prophet would suspect of cold-blooded murder.

Hadn't the kid saved Prophet's life a couple days ago?

Still, Prophet had been targeted by someone wielding a large-caliber rifle, and here the kid sat with his Sharps . . . on a sweat-soaked horse.

"You fired that rifle recently?" Prophet asked. He strode to the chestnut, grabbed the rifle from the kid's gloved hands, and sniffed the barrel.

"Why, sure I have," Ronnie said with mild indignation as Prophet's nose detected the bitter smell of burnt powder. "I just shot at a deer back over that ridge."

Prophet sent a glance behind the cantle of the kid's saddle, where a deer would have been draped if there'd been one. There wasn't. He had a feeling Ronnie didn't miss many shots.

"Where's the deer?"

"I gut-shot a buck. A wind gust took my bullet. Last I seen, he was headed that way." Ronnie nodded and flicked a finger to indicate a hillock rising in the southeast, just beyond a thin line of cottonwoods. "I was trackin' him when I heard the shootin'."

Prophet gave Ronnie back his rifle. Taking his own Winchester in his right hand, he grabbed the kid's deer-hide vest for purchase and swung up onto the chestnut's rump.

"Let's go find him," Prophet growled, his voice betraying his skepticism. "Maybe we'll find my horse in the process."

Ronnie spurred the chestnut into a swale and around the knoll's base. A half mile beyond the knoll, they came upon a six-point buck lying dead, one hind leg extended, amongst dock and cattails spiking a seep. The mule deer's snout and chest were blood-flecked. A large-caliber slug had torn a hole through its charcoal-colored belly.

"There he is," Ronnie said, reining the horse to a halt. "I was afraid I'd lose him in the river bed yonder."

Prophet nibbled his cheek. He doubted Ronnie could have shot at him *and* downed a deer in the space of a half hour. As Ronnie deftly and quickly dressed the buck, Prophet looked around at the rolling prairie dotted with wind-jostled sage and rabbit brush.

The shooter was probably long gone, but Prophet couldn't be sure he wouldn't return to try and finish the job. When the bounty hunter turned south and peered along the base of a low bench, he saw the gray mare casually cropping grass, about a hundred yards away.

Prophet jogged out to retrieve the horse. Twenty minutes later, he and Ronnie walked their mounts back toward Bitter Creek, riding abreast. Prophet told the kid about the shooting.

"You s'pose someone don't want you becomin' marshal of Bitter Creek?" the boy asked.

Prophet's neck tightened. "You know about that?"

"Mr. Kitchen told me this mornin', when I was buyin' eggs at the mercantile. Heck, everybody knows."

Prophet snorted. "Whole town probably knew before I did."

"Huh?"

"Never mind." Prophet saw no reason to go into the particulars of last night's debauch. Truth was, he deserved what he'd gotten. He was probably damn lucky he'd only been tagged with a badge. In Prophet's business, getting soused was a good way to get yourself greased by someone holding a grudge.

As he rode, he went over the faces he'd come to know in Bitter Creek—wondering which one wanted him dead. Anger tensed his jaw. He was trapped here now, tricked into taking a job he didn't want, shot at by someone who wouldn't show his face.

When he and the kid got back to Bitter Creek, Ronnie

headed to the café with his deer. Prophet watered the gray horse at a stock tank, then returned the mount to the alley behind the bank.

When he'd tied the horse to the iron wagon wheel, he took a gander around the alley, peering amidst the trash for any clue as to the gunman's identity. Seeing nothing the man might have dropped when he'd leapt from the roof to the shipping crates, Prophet decided to check out the roof itself.

When he'd piled the crates, climbed them, and hoisted himself onto the roof, he crept along the shakes, sliding his glance this way and that. Just behind the false facade jutting six feet above the roof, he crouched to get a better look at the shakes, hoping the man might have left a shell casing in the cracks between the shingles—anything offering some clue as to the bastard's identity.

Nothing.

He'd started to rise when something caught his eye. A rusty nail jutted from the side of the wooden facade. Wrapped around the nail head were several blue threads streaming out in the breeze.

Prophet removed the threads from the nail and inspected them between thumb and index finger. They'd been torn from faded blue cloth. They hadn't been wrapped very tightly around the nail, which meant they hadn't clung to the nail for more than a couple of hours, else the wind would have blown them away.

He'd have bet silver cartwheels against a carpetbagger's honor that the gunman had torn his shirt on the nail when he was levering shots at Prophet.

Pocketing the strands, the bounty hunter straightened and walked carefully back toward the rear of the bank, lowered himself to the crates, and leapt to the ground.

A woman's voice shot at him from his left. "Cousin Sarah! *There* you are!"

Prophet turned to see a diminutive old lady clad in

faded gingham approaching the gray mare. She turned her prune face, seared by at least seventy years of outdoor labor, to Prophet. "I was visiting Emma, and when I came out, Cousin Sarah was *gone*! I've been looking *all over*!"

"There she is," Prophet said, sheepish.

The woman ran her hand along the horse's sweaty coat and turned to Prophet, narrowing her eyes accusingly. "Why, she's been ridden!"

"Sure looks that way," Prophet said. "You'll wanna take her nice and slow on the way home."

He took the lady's arm and gently lifted her into the saddle, then wheeled and strode back to Main Street. He waited for a couple of burly miners to pass in a heavy ore wagon, a cream-colored bulldog barking in the box, before crossing the street and retrieving his shotgun from the boardwalk before the stage station. He was a little surprised to see the shotgun still lying where he'd left it, in a town with Bitter Creek's reputation for outlawry.

He stood on the boardwalk before the closed station house, gazing at the sparse wagon traffic passing before him—one-horse spring wagons and a few buggies driven by ranch women no doubt heading for one of Bitter Creek's two grocery stores.

A few horses were tied to the hitch racks before the two saloons—the American and the Mother Lode. A big Studebaker was parked before the feed store, and several men dressed in range clothes were loading fifty-pound oat sacks.

Prophet's brain registered little of it. He was too busy trying to figure out who wanted him dead. Not that it was all that bizarre. Bounty hunters made plenty of enemies. But something in his gut told him that this attempt on his hide had nothing to do with bounty hunting.

His stomach rumbled, and he suddenly realized he hadn't had breakfast.

Deciding to ponder his problems later—including what to do about the marshal's star he could still feel in his denim's pocket—he headed east up the street. He'd just stepped off the boardwalk fronting Polk's Health Tonic and Drug Emporium when a man spoke on his left.

"What was all the shootin' about earlier, Mr. Prophet?"

Prophet turned to see the mild-faced Wallace Polk standing on his store's front step. The weather had warmed, and the door was propped open to the breeze. Polk wore a white smock and bowler hat. His fair cheeks were still red from the sunburn he'd incurred on the Scanlons' trail.

"You tell me, Mr. Polk."

Polk's cheeks flushed behind the tan. He wrinkled his eyes.

"Forget it," Prophet said. "I'm just owly 'cause some-one took a shot at me and ran like a yellow-bellied dung beetle. I'll feel better once I get some food in my gut."

Polk looked concerned. "Took a shot at you? And you have no idea who it was?"

"Man in a blue shirt's all I know." Prophet looked around. Half the men going in and out of the stores and the land office wore blue shirts. Glancing back at Polk, Prophet grunted and continued angling across the street.

He turned the corner at the blacksmith shop and headed south to Gertrude's Good Food—a white frame house with a shabby barn out back. He opened the screen door and heard Ronnie Williams and a woman talking in the kitchen. They were discussing the deer. The woman had a German accent.

Gertrude, no doubt. He'd seen her before but had never learned her name.

It was late morning, so Prophet had his choice of the dozen or so tables covered with red and white oilcloth, several still bearing dirty breakfast dishes. When he'd doffed his hat and sat down, a full-hipped woman with an attractive, oval face and thick red hair stepped into the room.

"Ah, the new marshal!" she said in her German accent. "No?"

"No."

"No? I thought . . ."

"Ma'am, I'm so hungry my stomach thinks my throat's been cut, but I don't have a plug nickel to my name. If you'd—"

"You are Mr. Prophet, no?"

He sighed. "I'm Prophet."

She reached back inside the kitchen, produced a small brown envelope, and walked to Prophet's table, her swinging hips snapping the stained apron about her thighs. She was large but graceful, and her face and neck were flushed from serving the morning breakfast crowd.

Her white blouse was open at the neck, and her full breasts strained against the cloth. She exuded a raw sensuality as she smiled and set the envelope on the oilcloth, her voice a little breathless.

"Mr. Crumb left this."

Prophet picked up the envelope, upon which his name had been penciled. Inside was a note and a small sheaf of greenbacks. Prophet opened the note:

> *Mr. Prophet, I am deeply indebted to you for*
> *accepting the marshal's job on a temporary basis. By*
> *the time you read this, I'll have ridden out to talk to a*
> *man about taking the job permanently. With luck, I*
> *should have a full-time marshal in place in a couple*
> *of weeks. Enclosed find two hundred dollars. Your*
> *reward money for the Thorson-Mahoney Gang as*
> *well as the Scanlon Gang should be wired here soon.*
> *I intend to be back to Bitter Creek in a few days.*
> *Again, your help in this trying time is very much*
> *appreciated.*
>
> > *Gratefully and humbly yours,*
> > *Henry Crumb, Bitter Creek Mayor*
>
> *P.S. I hope the hangover is not overly severe, ha.*

Prophet threw the note and the money on the table. "Damn it all!"

The woman's brown eyes snapped wide, and her jaw dropped. "What is wrong—you don't like?"

Just then, Ronnie Williams stuck his head through the kitchen door. "Proph? I thought I heard your voice. What's wrong?"

Prophet's eyes narrowed. Adding to his quagmire of problems, the kid was indeed wearing a shirt of the same faded blue as the threads he'd found on the nail.

12

IT WAS NOT to Lou Prophet's credit that when faced with a surfeit of perplexing problems he often turned to whiskey and women.

The predicament of the ambush and of the marshal's job he seemed to have been hornswoggled into accepting were certainly not going to be decided on their own. But after he'd finished breakfast, he told the German woman who ran the restaurant, by way of small talk, that he was heading over to the bathhouse for a hot dip.

She responded by inviting him to take a dip with her in the pantry she'd turned into a bathroom complete with big porcelain tub and a small stove with a copper boiler.

Her devilish smile set off fireworks in the large, brown eyes flicking across his wide chest. Cheeks flushed and damp, with wisps of cherry-red hair sticking to them, she said in stilted English, "I am closing until four this afternoon, and vy vaste vater, no?"

Never a man to argue with a woman's good sense, Prophet followed the girl, whose name he learned was Frieda, granddaughter of the late Gertrude, into the pantry.

Waiting for the water to boil, they stripped and made love on their clothes, Prophet grunting bearlike between the girl's spread knees, her ankles crossed on his back, her hands pulling at his hair.

When they finished, Frieda donned Prophet's hat with a joyous trill, then poured a steaming bath tempered with cold water from the kitchen pump.

She tested the water with a toe, took Prophet's hand, and in a minute they both stood in the tub. Prophet soaped Frieda from behind, massaging her large, pendulous breasts with slow strokes of the perfumed soap, gradually working his way down to her soft, slightly swollen belly, to her thighs . . . and then the insides of the thighs to the silky nap between her legs.

She swooned back against him, so that he practically had to hold her up with one hand while he bathed her with the other, covering every inch of her big, smooth, hot body with the soap.

She reached above her head, moaning and caressing his jaws and clutching his shoulders as though clinging to a life raft in a raging, boiling sea.

"Goot enough for now. Now, my turn," she said throatily, twisting around to him, taking the soap as she kissed him.

She opened her mouth, stuck her warm tongue between his lips, and lapped his teeth as she scrubbed his broad shoulder blades, hard as a smithy's anvil. She kneaded the muscles with her knuckles and thumbs, pushing and grunting, her hands owning a bread baker's strength.

Her pinching, probing, soothing hands worked down his back, then came around to his belly. She briefly stuck a finger into his belly button and tittered.

Then both hands were again caressing, moving higher to the stonelike slabs of his chest. She pinched at the nipples and pressed the heels of her hands against the muscle tapering into the sloping, hublike shoulders.

Suddenly, she fell against him, nibbling his neck while

her hands closed around his jutting tool, exploring like a blind person learning a hammer by touch. She worked him into a delirious, near-catatonic state, and when the last few rational cells in his brain realized they'd better sit before they fell, he drew her down with him into the water.

Quickly, she straddled him, or tried to. The tub was bigger than any he'd seen beyond San Francisco and St. Louis, but there wasn't straddling room. She sat atop him, leaned back, and draped her feet over the sides. He grabbed her fleshy butt cheeks in both hands and drew her onto him. She made a noise that anyone passing the window might have misconstrued as a guttural cry of shock and horror as he plunged deep within her liquid, satin depths.

He pistoned her back and forth, up and down, between his raised knees. When they were finished, there was barely two gallons of water left in the tub.

"We made one hell of a mess on your floor there, Frieda," he said when he'd caught his breath.

She was leaning back, as he was, against her end of the tub. Glancing at the floor, she said, "It vas vorth every drop!"

"It's been a while, hasn't it?"

"Over two years."

While they lounged, legs entwined, Prophet learned that Frieda was only twenty-four, but she'd been married twice, once before she'd come out West with her grandparents, and once after. The first husband, twenty years her senior, had killed himself during the stock market troubles of the early '70s.

She'd met her second husband in Bitter Creek. A young farmer from north of town, he and Frieda had been married two months when he'd gotten drunk in the Mother Lode and gotten his throat cut by the shirttail cousin of a prominent Cheyenne businessman he'd played poker with.

Her grandparents had died of pneumonia last year, within two weeks of each other, leaving her alone to tend the restaurant.

"Lonely place for a pretty, needful young woman," Prophet said wistfully. She was nibbling his ankle like a ham bone. "Ever thought of packin' it in?"

She looked at him. "Pack it in?"

"You know—hightail it for higher ground? Leave?"

"I can't leave," she said as if he'd just suggested she turn cartwheels down Main Street. "My grandparents left me vith too many debts."

Prophet shrugged. "Sell out. Let the buyer assume your debts."

She looked at him slack-faced, as if wondering if he was being serious. "You don't know much about Bitter Creek—do you, Lou?"

"I reckon not. And though I have a feelin' it won't be good for me, I got a bad itch to know."

"If you vear that badge, take Mr. Crumb's two hundred dollars, you vill know soon enough."

He was about to ask her what she meant by that when hushed voices rose beyond the room's single window, followed by the unmistakable rasp of a revolver being cocked.

Fifteen minutes ago, two riders rode into Bitter Creek from the south, wending their way between shanties and piles of split cordwood, scattering chickens and setting several dogs to barking.

One of the riders, Leo Embry, was tall and thin, in his early twenties, with a hard-jawed, expressionless face. A new, wide-brimmed, cream Stetson sat at a rakish angle atop his head.

Embry wore a yellow-and-red checked shirt and a silver-plated Remington low on his right hip, the holster thonged just above his thigh. The shirt, gun, and holster were new as well. Embry had bought the works in the Bitter Creek mercantile three months ago, when he'd decided to become a gunslick, like his first cousin, Pike Thorson.

The other rider was a kid in his mid-teens named Gaelin Murphy, an orphan who swamped out saloons and mucked out livery stalls for spare pocket jingle, meals, and an occasional place in which to throw down his army blanket.

He wore torn denims and a faded undershirt beneath a vest sewn from elk hide. A wool watch cap sat low on his freckled forehead, his corn-yellow hair poking out from underneath the cap, soft as goose down. Fine yellow whiskers ran down from his sideburns, thinning to nothing along his jaw. A sparse yellow mustache rode atop his mouth, barely visible until the sun hit it right, causing individual strands to glisten.

He wore a battered .38 in a soft leather holster flapping loose against his thigh. He kicked the ribs of his old nag, trying to keep up with the fine, broad-chested paint of his steely-eyed companion who rode taut-backed in his saddle, his right hand caressing the grips of his glistening .44.

Young Gaelin had ridden out to the little ten-cow ranch where Leo Embry worked with his uncles when he wasn't practicing his fast draw against trash heap rats and vegetable tins. Gaelin had relayed to Embry the news of the Thorson-Mahoney Gang's demise at the hand of a Rebel bounty hunter named Prophet.

Embry had been young Gaelin's hero since the time, a few months back, when he'd watched Embry pistol-whip a braggy gambler behind the Mother Lode Saloon before sending the man, tied belly-down across his saddle, galloping out of town.

Now the two riders ducked under a clothesline, trotted through the wind-buffeting trash of a vacant lot, and reined to a halt on Main Street. The older of the two swung his hard expression up and down the street, squinting and rolling his eyes around in their sockets.

"He'd be in a saloon, no doubt," the younger man said, keeping his voice low and serious, trying to sound as tough as his older companion looked.

"Maybe, maybe not," Embry muttered self-importantly after a moment, raking his squinting gaze along the boardwalks.

It was midday, and farm and ranch wagons clattered along the wide, rutted Main Street, which was only three blocks long and intersected by two side streets. Horsebackers rode in twos and threes—drifters mostly, with a few ranch hands here and there, heading for the harness shop, feed store, or mercantile, on errands for their employers.

It was quiet by Bitter Creek's night standards, but several sporting girls plied their scantily clad wares from saloon balconies. One—a toothless half-breed—stood on a street corner, flashing her bare breasts at passing riders, a few of whom hooted and yelled obscenities while others simply ignored her. "Mad Mary" had been working the same corner so long that she'd become invisible to all but strangers.

Young Gaelin Murphy stared at her, revulsion spoking his eyes and curling his thin upper lip.

Leo Embry reached out to swat his shoulder. "You get you a good eyeful, Gaelin, my boy," he said with mocking humor. "You and her'll be playin' slap 'n' tickle next month."

The younger lad's lip twitched as he stared. "I don't want nothin' to do with that buggy half-breed. Why, she'd curl the tail of a gut-wagon cur."

"No?"

The older lad's steely stare was fastened on the creature performing a macabre, half-clad two-step with an awning post. Opening her hide dress with one hand, she extended her other arm to two passing riders, hooking her fingers and cackling like a Halloween ghoul.

Strands of long, gray-black hair framed her wide, flat face and the breasts that hung to her belly, like water flasks, the nipples tilted toward her feet.

"I'll admit she ain't no Lillie Langtry, but limber your pecker up, boy," Embry continued. "Every kid in the county has to give her a poke when he turns seventeen. Those are the rules. Course I threw my guts up afterwards and was pickin' bugs from my crotch for the next two months, but by God, I did it!"

Somehow, he chuckled without smiling, only jerking his shoulders slightly and making soft snorting sounds. He reined his horse left up Main Street, around a two-seater buggy parked before the gunsmith shop.

Inwardly recoiling at the prospect of coupling with Mad Mary, but figuring if Embry did it, then by God he'd do it too, Gaelin gigged his nag after the handsome paint, tracing a path through the buckboards and mining drays. The riders shuttled their gazes from one side of the street to the other, then reined up before Hobbs' Livery Stables and Feed Barn.

Embry turned to Gaelin, his expression grim. "No sign of the son of a bitch, eh?"

Gaelin shook his head. "Prob'ly in one of the whorehouses."

"I'll find him," Embry said, leading his horse up the long ramp, through the barn's gaping doors, and into the cool, dusky interior rife with animal smells.

Embry called into the shadows, down the central alley lined with three leather-topped buggies and several buckboards, tongues drooping to the hay-strewn, dung-littered floor. A figure stepped out of the shadows wielding a pitchfork—a fat youngster with freckles, deep-sunk eyes, and a shaved scalp. He wore tattered overalls over his fish-belly-white torso that boasted breasts the size of a chubby girl in her teens.

"Hey, Leo," he said, running his admiring gaze up and down the young gunslick's natty duds, letting his eyes linger on the Remington in Embry's holster. He swallowed with emotion. "You gonna . . . you gonna . . . ?"

"You know what I'm here for, Fats," Embry said coolly. "You seen the son of a bitch lately?"

Fats nodded. "'Bout an hour ago, I seen him headin' for Gert's. I told Richy Searls to give a coyote yell if he seen him leave, and I ain't heard nothin' so far. . . ."

His expression all business, Embry dug in his pocket and flipped a nickel at Fats, who snapped it expertly out of the air and grinned.

"Unsaddle our horses and curry 'em good. Give 'em plenty of water and oats. I'll be back in an hour."

"Uh . . . what about Mr. Crumb?"

Embry knew the mayor was out of town, but he said snidely, "Fuck Mr. Crumb."

He turned, glanced at Gaelin meaningfully, then sauntered down the ramp, his thumbs hooked inside his cartridge belt.

"Be careful, Leo," Fats called, holding the reins of Embry's paint with one hand and tossing the nickel in the air with the other. "I mean, you heard what he did to the gang . . . him and that girl . . ."

"Yeah, I heard what he done," Embry grumbled, turning at the end of the ramp and heading down Main Street.

Gaelin hurried after him while holding his pistol against his thigh. Gaelin caught up to the older lad but had to jog every fourth step to keep up as Embry's legs were several inches longer than the boy's.

"What do you think, Embry? Can we take the son of a bitch?"

"My cousin went down," Embry said tightly, staring straight ahead, chin down, the brim of his hat hiding his eyes. "I can take—" He jerked a look at the youngster. "What do you mean 'we'?"

"I wanna help, Leo. I wanna be a famous gunman, just like you. I'll play your back."

"Play my . . . ?" Embry frowned, then sneered. "You mean, back my play."

"Can I, Leo?"

Embry looked at the youngster critically, enjoying the

kid's admiring, beseeching gaze. He pretended to think about it.

Actually, he'd already made up his mind. He'd never faced a short-trigger man before, and a cold knot of fear tightened just above his belt buckle. He wouldn't have admitted such a thing in a million years, but he liked the idea of having someone—even a snot-nosed brat with a rusty .38—back his play.

"I reckon you can tag along," he said finally, nodding dully. "But stay behind me, and for chrissakes, don't make any noise! I gotta warn you, though, it's gonna be bloody."

"Blood don't bother me, Leo," the kid said, one hand on his gun grips. "You won't be sorry, Leo—I promise!"

Embry snorted and said nothing to his young partner, maintaining a hard expression as he and Gaelin approached the café.

Embry paused in the yard, scrutinizing the one-and-a-half-story clapboard-and-whitewashed structure with a few geraniums and yucca planted around the foundation, rubbing his jaw thoughtfully.

"What we gonna do? How we gonna play it?"

"Follow me and keep your mouth shut."

They walked Indian-file around the south side of the building, ducking under two windows. At the café's rear, Embry sidled up to the first sashed window and edged a quick look inside.

Turning to Gaelin standing behind him, back to the shack's wall, he shook his head. He ducked under the window and, young Gaelin aping his every step and move, edged to the next window, on the other side of a small door.

Embry removed his hat, turned to the building, and edged his left eye across the frame and over the glass. Seeing two figures inside, he jerked his eye back behind the wall, took a deep, calming breath, and stole another look.

Inside the small room behind the foggy window glass, a small iron stove stood against the left wall, topped with a steaming copper kettle. Before the stove, two people sat facing each other in a big, porcelain tub.

Embry couldn't see clearly because of the moisture, but the two appeared to be relaxing, heads thrown back on their shoulders. Squinting, he saw that one was the big bounty hunter; the other was Frieda Schwartzenberger.

Leo Embry snickered. His loins twitched. He'd always fantasized about rolling the big, sexy German woman, but whenever he'd tried flirting with her, she'd merely laughed and told him to come back when the green was off his horns.

His mouth tightened as jealousy now mixed with anger.

Rolling his glance away from the tub, Embry saw a pistol and cartridge belt hanging from a wall hook, to the left of and above a sawed-off shotgun and a Winchester '73.

Embry turned to Gaelin, watching him nervously.

"Wait here," he whispered. "Keep your head down so they don't see you. When you hear me kick that inside door, you go in through there." He gestured to the small back door leading into the pantry. "And for godsakes, watch where you aim that old blunderbuss of yours."

"You got it, Embry."

The older lad walked around to the front and entered the café by the main door. He walked through the tables upon which midday sunlight lay, washing in through the windows Frieda kept clean as crystal.

Pushing through the swinging door, he entered the kitchen, saw the skinned deer carcass hanging in the back, near a six-foot plank table, then stepped past the big black range to a door in the left wall. His nostrils twitched at the heavy smell of onions emanating from a stew pot simmering on the range.

Embry considered the door for a moment, feeling his heart thumping heavily, then quickly, his skin tingling. He took a deep breath and smiled, hearing his name tossed around the saloons that night. Soon, it would make it to

Cheyenne and points north and south along the Burlington Northern Line. Everyone from lawmen to line girls would be kissing his butt shortly.

No more brush-popping calves and year-old heifers out at his uncle's ten-cow spread north of the Buckskin Hills . . . No, sir, no more of that bullshit for Leo Embry!

Eventually, high-rollers would be calling for him . . . men who needed other men turned beneath the sod.

Eyes bright, lips pulled back from his teeth, barely able to choke down the gleeful chuckle rising in his chest, Embry lifted one of the tooled boots he was still paying for and kicked the door.

It slammed back against the wall as Embry rushed inside, gun extended. A sudden, inexplicable burning engulfed him.

"Ahhhhhhhhhh!" he screamed. His face, head, and shoulders burned as though he'd been dunked in an acid vat.

Looking down, he saw steaming water washing over the floorboards, soaking his boots. The skin of his scalp felt as though it were punctured by a million sharp pins. He stumbled forward, screaming and firing the Remington blindly, squeezing his eyes closed against the burn.

Naked and still wet from the bath, Lou Prophet watched from a kneeling position beside the stove. He held his cocked .45 in his right hand.

He'd heard the hushed voices outside the bathhouse window and seen the figures through the cracks between the vertical siding planks. Quickly but quietly, he and Frieda had slipped out of the tub. She'd retreated to the kitchen while he'd propped the boiling pot on the narrow shelf above the door, connecting its handle to the doorknob with twine he'd found in his jeans pocket.

Now he winced as his would-be attacker's face turned the red of a Georgia sunset. The kid dropped his revolver, lifted his chin to the ceiling, and screamed.

Frieda appeared behind him, clad in a checked robe and

wielding an iron fry pan. "Take that, you crazy pup!" she cried and swung the pan forward, connecting solidly with the back of the kid's head.

Prophet winced as the young man fell face-forward on the wet puncheons, out like a blown candle.

The door to Prophet's right opened suddenly. Prophet turned to see another kid, around sixteen, bolt forward with an old .38 held before him. Seeing his comatose partner on the other side of the tub, the kid froze and stared.

"Leo!" he screamed.

"Hold it right there, kid," Prophet said, standing and bringing his .45 to bear on the youngster.

The kid turned to see the tall, naked bounty hunter standing before the stove. The kid's eyes found the .45's yawning maw.

His hand opened and his .38 dropped to the floorboards. The kid stumbled back, arms spread and eyes wide, as though he'd just stepped on a coiled rattler.

Then he stood there, shivering, face bleaching, staring at Prophet's .45. Piss dribbled down his leg to puddle around the soles of his frayed brogans.

Prophet had just held up his left hand to calm the kid when the youngster gave another shrill cry, turned, and bolted out the door. Prophet stepped to the door and looked out. The kid was running straight out through the weeds behind the café, toward the willows and cottonwoods lining the distant ravine.

The kid ran hard, throwing his arms up high.

"*Ja!*" said Frieda, throwing her head back and cackling. "Look at him go!"

13

PROPHET SAT IN the jailhouse and studied the badge in his hand.

The young man who'd tried to ambush him, whose name Frieda had informed him was Leo Embry, was sleeping in one of the three gloomy cells behind him. He was too unconscious to even snore, but Prophet heard him utter a painful groan now and then.

The local medico, a portly, rheumy-eyed Dr. Beamer, who stank of stale beer and laudanum, had checked the kid out and wrapped a white bandage around Embry's head, then smacked his lips with the anticipation of an imminent libation and angled across the street to the Mother Lode.

Frieda had tattooed Embry with such force that the doctor thought he'd probably sleep until tomorrow, or wish he'd had. He had a bump on the back of his head the size of a hickory knot. The doctor said he'd probably have a headache as momentous as three military hangovers, and Beamer looked and smelled like a man who knew what he was talking about.

Prophet hadn't consciously decided to take the mar-

shal's job until he'd carried the kid halfway to the jailhouse. Drunk or not, he'd already accepted the position,
and he couldn't renege on the agreement.

Also, without Crumb's two hundred dollars, he'd be flat
broke until his reward money came in. He might as well wear
a badge than swamp saloons or shovel shit in the livery barn.

Besides, somebody didn't want him taking the job. And
that didn't sit well with the bounty hunter. He didn't want
the job himself, but he'd like to know who was willing to
drill him to keep him from taking it.

Somebody besides Leo Embry. Frieda had told Prophet
that Embry was merely a wet-behind-the-ears farm boy
who fancied himself the next Billy the Kid. She'd seen the
boy shoot in competition at summer picnics, and she
doubted he could hit a tomato can if the can was privy-
sized and Leo was sitting inside.

Whoever had shot at Prophet from the bank roof knew
what he was doing. If Prophet hadn't turned as the man had
fired, his shoulders would be looking mighty funny now,
minus their head. He didn't think Ronnie Williams was responsible. Why save Prophet's life only to take it later?

There was someone else in town who, for whatever reason, didn't want Prophet wearing a badge. Someone good
with a rifle, or at least someone who'd hired someone good
with a rifle. Someone smart enough not to have hired an in-
effectual miscreant like Leo Embry to do his dirty work.

Who?

Prophet tossed the tin star in the air, then pinned it just
above the left breast pocket of his buckskin tunic.

He had to chuckle as he caught a look at himself in the
cracked mirror over the washstand behind the door. He
wished Louisa could see him now. He wondered what his
two lawman friends, Owen McCreedy and Zeke McIlroy,
would say. They'd both have a good laugh, after all the
problems Prophet had had with badge-toters over the
years.

Well, he wouldn't be toting the Bitter Creek marshal's badge for long. As soon as Henry Crumb got back from his trip and the reward money arrived, he'd stuff a few fresh reward posters into his saddlebags and light a shuck for the owlhoot trail. By then, his bushwhacker would probably have attempted another bushwhack, and he and Prophet would have settled the matter once and for all. . . .

He glanced into the far west cell. Leo Embry lay flat on his back, one arm hanging straight off the cot and bobbing as he breathed. The kid's mouth was twisted painfully. The window over Leo's head was a barred, rectangular square of brassy, afternoon light, causing the bandage on the kid's bruised skull to glow as if from the misery within.

Satisfied the kid would be out for several more hours, Prophet grabbed his shotgun, donned his hat, and headed outside to familiarize himself with the town.

He was approaching the stage depot a few minutes later when five horseback riders rode toward him, silhouetted against the west-angling sun.

Prophet stopped and scrutinized the group as it passed the livery barn on the right side of Main and approached the harness shop on the left. They rode slowly on tall, muscular horses coated with trail dust—five hard-faced men wearing dusters, crisp Stetsons, and cowhide boots into which the cuffs of their black trousers were stuffed.

As the riders approached Prophet, several dusters blew back, revealing gold watch chains and well-tended pistols in oiled, hand-tooled holsters. Prophet saw a couple of shoulder rigs in addition to the hip holsters. Winchester rifles protruded from saddle boots jutting up beneath the riders' thighs.

A vein in Prophet's right temple twitched. These men looked to be every bit as much trouble as those in the Thorson-Mahoney and Scanlon Gangs. Each had the icy, arrogant look of an accomplished cold-steel artist.

One of riders on the right side of the pack saw Prophet,

and looked startled when he saw the badge on the bounty hunter's chest. He swatted the man beside him and indicated Prophet with a nod.

The other man turned his flinty gaze to the town's new lawman. Both men curled their lips into smiles and rode on.

As the group set a couple brindle curs to barking, the druggist, Polk, appeared under his store's wooden awning. The lean, mild-faced druggist regarded the group with interest. Several of the riders turned to him as they passed. The druggist held their gazes, then—was that a nod?

Prophet's brows furrowed as he watched the riders ride away, wondering at the unspoken communication between them and Polk. If that's what it had been. What business could they possibly have with the mild-mannered druggist?

Prophet was shuttling his gaze from the five-man group to the druggist when Polk turned toward him. Prophet knew the man had spotted him, but Polk jerked his head down, pretending he hadn't seen Prophet, and stepped back inside his store.

Prophet glowered eastward along Main, baffled. When the five riders turned into the hitch rack before one of the brothels, he nudged his hat up to scratch the back of his head. He turned and continued walking west.

"Marshal!" a shrill cry rose on his right. His right hand slapped the grips of his .45 and he turned.

But it was only the half-breed whore, Mad Mary, walking toward him between a billiard hall and an old, gray cabin. She drew a tattered, multicolored cape about her shoulders, giving Prophet a glimpse of her slack, brown breasts, permanently extended nipples drooping groundward.

Behind her, a young cowboy—apparently too young and down-at-the-heel to afford one of the town's more comely doves—was buttoning his baggy jeans. He glanced at Prophet, sheepish, then crouched to retrieve a worn pistol belt.

Wrapping the belt around his lean hips, the young

drover turned to the saddled horse standing ground-reined nearby. He swung into the saddle and, tossing one more sheepish glance behind, gigged the mouse-colored dun into a gallop across a hay field, heading north toward the creek and the low hills beyond.

"Miss Mary," Prophet said greeting the whore. They hadn't been introduced, but he'd seen her on the street, and during the long posse ride he'd heard several townsmen joking about her.

Walking toward him, she shook an admonishing finger and grinned, showing only two or three discolored teeth around her deeply-lined witch's face framed with long, coarse hair the color of a soiled gun rag.

"Wendigo here in Bitter Creek. Yes, yes, yes! Wendigo here, and he no like lawmen!"

Shaking her head and cackling, she brushed past him and angled off across the street, holding her ragged skirts above the men's high-button shoes she'd scavenged from some trash heap. One shoe was missing a heel, and it gave her a limp. A bearded farmer in a buckboard had to pull up to avoid hitting the whore.

"Damnit, Mary, I'm gonna flatten you yet!"

When she'd disappeared between the bank and the feed store on the other side of the street, the farmer cursed, returned his corncob pipe to his teeth, and shook the reins over his sway-backed mule, continuing east along Main.

Wendigo here and he no like lawmen! What had she meant by that? Did Mary know who'd tried to ambush him?

Beyond the livery barn, Prophet angled north, crossed a shallow ravine, and climbed a flat-topped hill of red gravel, sage, and yucca. It wasn't an overly high hill, but a steep one, and at the top he paused to catch his breath and curse himself for all the whiskey and cigarettes he mindlessly consumed.

He was swinging back to take a slow gander at the town when something caught his eye.

He turned northwest and tugged his hat brim low to shield his eyes from the fiery sun slipping into a notch between two rimrocks. On a mesa a hundred yards away lay a small cemetery in tall bromegrass, shaded by a single cedar. Several mourners stood before a fresh grave and a rough pine coffin, facing a minister holding an open Bible. Nearby were two buggies, a buckboard, and three saddle horses.

Prophet studied the solemn scene from under his Stetson's funneled brim, recognizing Fianna Whitman standing stiffly before the preacher.

The only other figures he could identify were those of the banker, Ralph Carmody, and Sorley Kitchen, the retired ranch cook who now painted houses and repaired pots and pans for a living.

The funeral had to be that of Marshal Whitman.

Prophet wondered why so few mourners had shown up. He counted less than a dozen people standing with the lawman's daughter. The preacher bent to scoop a handful of soil from the mound beside the grave. When he'd said a few more words and had traced a cross in the air, the mourners turned and started to walk slowly toward the horses and wagons.

Only a couple of people spoke to Fianna before she lifted her black skirts above her shoes, mounted a canopied buggy, and started along the faint cemetery trace toward the main trail to town. She looked terribly sad and alone, riding singly in that black, yellow-wheeled buggy. It pecked at Prophet for a long time. He turned it over in his head—just one more peculiarity in a town that seemed to grow them like weeds.

Finally, when the mourners had dispersed, he turned back to the task at hand. He wandered his gaze slowly down the town's main drag with its high false fronts and livery corrals.

He gave the town a slow study, picking out the places a

man might use to effect an ambush—the highest buildings, the narrowest alleys, the shadow pools around outside stairwells. A ravine angled behind the jailhouse to intersect with the main trail on the town's eastern edge. A sharpshooter could lay in there while Prophet was entering or leaving the jailhouse and pick him off cleanly.

He identified a few more spots to keep an eye on during the day, a few to avoid at night, and several horse trails a drygulcher might use for escape routes.

As the fast-falling sun gilded the Main Street storefronts, he headed back down the hill, loosing gravel behind his softly singing spurs, one hand on the butt of his .45, Mad Mary's shrill warning echoing in his ears.

He walked around the north end of town, then the south, pondering the situation here while keeping a close eye on his backtrail.

He stopped by a small cabin before which an old lady was removing wash from a line, her blue gingham dress blowing about her heavy legs as the evening breeze kicked up. An old man smoked a pipe on the porch while a mule cropped grass under a nearby ash.

"Ma'am, I'm wonderin' if you could point me to the Whitman home."

The old woman stared at Prophet dully, several ratty sheets clamped under an arm, a few clothespins in her teeth. The corners of her mouth pinched and her eyes narrowed, as if he'd just asked her where he could get his ashes hauled. Silently, she extended her free arm, indicating a white frame house on the other side of a cabin to the west.

"Much obliged," he said, pinching his hat brim to her.

The Whitman place was one of the biggest he'd seen in Bitter Creek so far—a neat, two-and-a-half-story, clapboard-and-frame house with a stone chimney abutting the east wall. There was a large, screened porch, a buggy shed and a stable out back, and a big yard with flowers and transplanted trees.

All in all, it was a nice setup for a lawman and a school-teacher. Too nice and damn odd. Prophet wondered if Whitman had blasted a few nuggets out of the mountains, or if there was some other reason he could afford such digs.

A black-and-white cat slinked under the porch as the bounty hunter walked through the rickety gate, mounted the brick steps, opened the screen door, and stepped onto the porch.

It was a full minute after he'd knocked on the inside door before slow footsteps sounded within.

Fianna Whitman didn't say anything when she opened the door, just stood there in the dark foyer, arching an eye-brow bemusedly, one hand on the knob. She'd changed from the black dress she'd worn to the funeral to a long, slitted nightgown over which she wore a blue silk wrapper.

She was prettier than he'd remembered, with big, brown eyes and a wide mouth. Her eyes were a little glassy and boldly insinuating.

She'd let her hair down, the auburn curls curving over her shoulder to hang down beside her right breast, the top of which was revealed by the low-cut gown and the wrap-per curving open at her chest.

The way she regarded Prophet, as though she'd been ex-pecting him, made him half-wonder if he'd taken a wrong turn and found himself at a whorehouse.

"Ma'am," Prophet said, his hat in his hands, uncertain what to say now that he was here.

He'd come because he honestly felt sorry for her, hav-ing seen how few mourners had shown up at the funeral. But he was also hoping to find out why so few of Bitter Creek's citizens had seen fit to attend the ceremony. He thought it might have something to do with the apprehen-sion Whitman had voiced about the town.

"I thought I'd pay my respects. I saw the funeral was to-day, and—"

"Yes, I saw you on the hill, Mr. Prophet. Why didn't you join us? The more the merrier."

She smiled wryly, stepped back, and drew the door wide. "Won't you come in?"

"Thank you." But as he stepped into the foyer, he saw that she was barefoot, and he suddenly felt out of place. The lady wasn't dressed for company. He looked at her. "Are you sure, ma'am? Looks like you're ready for bed."

A loud clock ticked somewhere. A plush runner lay beneath his boots, the wood floor on either side of it polished to a high, oak gloss.

"Of course I'm sure, Mr. Prophet." He detected a thickness to her voice, as though she'd been drinking. When she closed the door, she leaned a little too far toward it. She had to steady herself against it before she turned to him with that funny smile still quirking her lips, lending a leer to her eyes. "I don't get many visitors."

Taken aback by her tipsy boldness, he took a moment to formulate his question. "On a day like this, ma'am? I'd have thought . . ."

"Don't think, Mr. Prophet. That's rule one when working for Henry Crumb."

"I don't exactly work for Crumb," he said, her tone having set him back on his heels. "As a matter of fact, I was pretty much tricked into the job."

"Oh?" she said, as though she didn't believe it, making him feel even more resentful. "How much money did he offer?"

He told her.

"There'll be more where that came from."

He was about to tell her there would be no more money, because he'd be on the trail out of here as soon as Crumb returned with his new lawman, but before he could open his mouth to respond, she said, "Join me for a drink?"

Her tone had changed, her voice suddenly soft and velvety, the smile no longer as much leering as coquettish. He'd always been a sucker for whiskey and coquettes, especially underdressed coquettes.

He glanced at her bare feet, at the robe she did little to keep closed. "I'd have one as long as I'm not intrudin'. I really just stopped to pay my respects and to see if you needed any help. I know how it must be, your pa suddenly gone. . . ."

She'd started moving into the foyer's dusky shadows. She turned her head and looked at him, smiling again, subtly devilish, running her gaze up and down his tall, broad frame, making him self-conscious.

"What I need, Mr. Prophet," she said, pausing, then continuing as she turned and began moving down the foyer again, "is another drink. Come . . . right this way . . ."

He followed her a few feet down the hall and into the parlor opening off to the left. No lights had been lit in here either. She strolled to a table on which sat several bottles and tumblers. She turned one of the tumblers right side up.

"Bourbon or rye?"

"What are you drinking?" He'd seen the glass on a low table beside a damask-covered rocker. An open cigar box sat beside it, but it didn't look like cigars inside.

"Bourbon. It's the best—a gift from Dad's employer last Christmas."

Fianna's voice acquired a sarcastic, flippant tone. "Dad's taste always ran to beer or the coffin varnish Burt Carr serves at the Mother Lode." She smiled. "So I drink Henry Crumb's bourbon. Acquired quite a taste for it, in fact," she added with a throaty laugh.

She held up the bottle to Prophet, gave it a little jiggle, sloshing the liquid around. He stood just inside the door, his hat in his hands, watching the girl with interest.

When he'd seen her earlier, he hadn't taken her for a drinker. He'd thought schoolteachers, like ministers, didn't imbibe. But in the soft light through the open window behind her, he saw that only a few fingers of bourbon remained in the bottle.

"Since you recommend it, I'll try the bourbon," he said, though his tastes ran more to beer and rye.

He glanced around at the soft sofa against the opposite wall, the several comfortable chairs and fancy lamps sitting on the expensive wooden tables that must have been shipped in from Denver or Cheyenne. To his left stood a bookcase crammed with books.

Again, he was impressed and puzzled by the house. It was the kind of home a well-to-do businessman might own.

"Nice place you have here," he observed when, after handing him his drink, she'd directed him to a chair near hers.

She dropped into her own chair, curling one leg beneath her. Her robe and nightgown parted to reveal a long, creamy thigh and knee—too much skin to make the revelation an accident. "I can light a lamp if you want," she said. "I guess it would be proper."

Prophet quirked a brow at the thigh, feeling his tongue grow thick. He cleared his throat. "Only . . . only if you want one, ma'am."

"No," she said, sipping her drink. "I like the dark. Did my neighbor, Mrs. Dane, see you? She'd think it totally improper for me to be entertaining a man alone and not even lighting a lamp."

"I reckon," Prophet said, feeling as out of place as a bear in a millinery shop, wishing he hadn't come.

She was drunk and lonely, and her blood was running high. He had a feeling it always ran a little high, but her father's death must have turned up the heat. Before he came, he'd thought he'd drink some coffee with her, maybe cut some wood for her, move some boxes, get some questions answered, and leave.

But it was already a more complicated visit—with that thigh and fully half of one breast staring at him boldly, daring him to move in on her.

In that regard, it was like everything else in this damn town. Complicated, bewildering, hard to refuse. It was like quicksand, sucking you down.

He couldn't wait to ride Mean and Ugly along some remote mountain trail, far away from this devil's lair. Towns—even normal towns—were too damn complicated.

"Yes, it is a nice place," she finally responded to his remark, glancing around thoughtfully. "You'll have a place like it soon. You'll need a woman to dress it up for you. Do you have one of those yet, Mr. Prophet?"

Again, before he could draw responsive air across his vocal cords, she said, "Miss Schwartzenberger perhaps?" She smiled. "She's a very good cook, just like her grandmother."

Prophet's ears warmed again, and his chest drew taut. He scowled. "Miss Whitman—"

"Call me Fianna."

"Fianna, I'm sorry if I'm bein' too forward, but can I ask you just what in the hell you're talking about?"

She smiled as though enjoying his vexation, but asked coyly, "What do you mean?"

"How could a small-town lawman possibly afford a house like this? I assume you and your father brought money from back East, or you found gold up in the mountains."

As she studied him from fifteen feet away, her playful smirk gradually faded. She threw back the last of her drink. As she lowered the glass in her right hand, her smile was replaced by a shrewd expression, her eyes narrowing. "If Mr. Crumb hasn't told you, he will soon enough."

"Are you suggesting I'd do something illegal?"

"I'm suggesting you're made of the same flesh and blood as my father."

Her eyes hardened. Her shoulders slumped and she exhaled a long draft of air. A sob carried on it, or what sounded like a sob. A soft, mournful wail. She was an unexpectedly pricked balloon. Her face crumpled, her mouth quivering. She lowered her head, not making any sound until she lifted it again. She inhaled and sniffed.

"Oh, damnit!" she said and struggled up from her seat. More unsteadily than before, letting the wrapper flap around her long legs, she walked to the table, tipped several more fingers of bourbon into her glass, and set the empty bottle down hard.

She straightened, stiffened, threw her head back, and sobbed louder this time. She grabbed her shoulders as if chilled to the bone and lowered her chin to her chest. She stood there, shuddering and sobbing, making soft crying sounds.

Prophet sat wondering what to do, wondering what he should say, feeling like he'd just wandered into some drama halfway through the last act.

Finally, cursing under his breath, he set his drink down, stood, and walked over to her. He regarded the back of her head indecisively, feeling even more awkward than before, not sure how much of her emotion was genuine and how much was the bourbon.

Either way, he'd always had a hard time comforting distraught women. Whatever he said always seemed to be the wrong thing.

When he placed his hands on her shoulders, she instantly quit sobbing and melted back against him, canting her head against his chest. Her body was warm and soft beneath the wrapper and nightgown, and it seemed to mold to his, as if wanting to draw his large body around her like a quilt.

She smelled of bourbon and summer rain. When she turned her head to press her cheek against his chest, he felt the dampness of her tears through his shirt.

"Miss Fianna," he said, shaking his head and wincing, "I really just wanted—"

Prophet heard the squawk of a floorboard a second before he saw a gun barrel glint in the doorway. A man's voice rose with exasperation. "Fianna!"

14

WITH A GASP, the girl jerked her head toward the door.

A man stood silhouetted against the frame, a pistol extended in his right hand. In the murky light, Prophet couldn't make out his face. But he was slender and wore a cream shirt, brown vest, and dark trousers. Garters ringed his arms just above his elbows.

Fianna snapped, "Wallace!"

Prophet scowled, befuddled. Wallace *Polk*?

The man mumbled incoherently as, stepping slowly forward, he kept the pistol extended at Prophet—a snub-nosed Bisley, it appeared. Probably a .38.

Prophet turned toward him, keeping his left hand on the girl, ready to jerk her behind him. Sure enough—Wallace Polk, the town druggist, had a .38 pointed right at his head. As the man approached, Prophet saw the rheumy blue eyes of Wallace Polk, minus their mildness. Snarling and shivering before him, like Polk's evil twin, the man extended the pistol and thumbed back the hammer.

Prophet stared down the bore, wide-eyed. "Easy, Polk.

Better give that to me. Don't want no one gettin' hurt here now, do we?"

Prophet extended his right hand half-defensively, only half-hoping Polk would give him the gun.

"I saw you walking this way," Polk spit through gritted teeth. His voice had lost its customary timidity and politeness. "Just knew what you had on your sexually depraved mind."

Prophet's brow arched. "Sexually depraved?"

"Weren't satisfied with Frieda Schwartzenberger, eh? Decided to comfort the sheriff's grieving daughter?"

Prophet winced as one part of his brain wondered if his bath with Frieda was known throughout the entire county, while the other tried to grasp Polk's presence here in Fianna's parlor, snarling like a wolf over a deer bone.

Wallace Polk with his liquid blue eyes and timid grin.

Prophet's brain revolted at the image.

Was this whole town crazy? Maybe the place really had been hexed by an Indian spirit, as Mad Mary had insinuated.

Meanwhile, he tore his eyes from Polk's crazed face to stare down the Bisley's gaping bore, awaiting and dreading the blossoming report, the bullet carving a messy hole through his brain.

So this was where it ended. After all the badmen he'd hauled to justice, he was going to be taken down by a mild-mannered, crazed druggist with a burr under his saddle for a crazed brunette.

Who would tell Louisa? She would sure be disgusted with him, after she got over the heartbreak.

Prophet's brain recoiled again. Was he getting as crazy as everyone else around here? He wasn't going to just stand here and get shot by a druggist.

"Polk, goddamnit, there's nothing goin' on between me and Fianna. Put down that gun!"

"Wallace, you put that gun down this instant!" Fianna ordered, her voice quaking slightly.

Polk didn't seem to hear them. Eyes so wide the whites glowed, he moved toward Prophet across the room, one slow step at a time. He kept the gun extended at Prophet's face, his hand shaking. Behind the gun, his thin lips formed a snarl. Sweat dribbled down his cheeks.

He stopped ten feet away. "I should've known you'd prey on our women. That's what men like you do, isn't it? Lone wolf, come to town. Come to take all the women. I tried to tell Henry—"

"Wallace—"

Polk's pinched voice cut her off. "He's just taking advantage of your sorrow. I'd have been at the funeral, but you know how people talk."

"Wallace I didn't *want* you at the funeral. I've told you, whatever there might have been between us . . . it's over now. . . ."

He hadn't heard a word of it. He jerked the gun at Prophet, but spoke to her. "I won't hold this against you . . . at a time like this. I know it's me you love."

He paused, sniffed as though he had pepper in his nose, then shifted his eerily bright, narrowed eyes back to Prophet. He steadied the gun. His hand shook.

"Polk, no!" shouted Prophet.

"You *bastard*!"

The gun barked. In the close quarters, it sounded like a cannon. Instinctively, Prophet threw himself against the girl. She cried out as she slammed into the table, knocking over glasses and bottles.

Though fired from only ten feet away, the bullet had somehow missed him.

Prophet swung his left arm toward Polk. His hand closed on the man's forearm, then slid to the gun. As he wrenched it free of the druggist's grip, he straightened and leveled a left jab at the man's face, connecting solidly with cheekbone.

Polk gave a cry and stumbled sideways and back before

dropping to his knees. He lunged forward, as though trying to bolt to his feet, but reconsidered and cowered on his haunches. His shoulders fell as he lowered his head in defeat, brought his hands to his face, and sobbed.

"Goddamn you!"

"Took the words right out of my mouth," Prophet said, breathing hard, adrenaline still raging in his veins.

His glance found the small, round hole in the wall behind where he'd been standing when Polk had fired. Polk's quivering hand had nudged the bullet a hair left.

Prophet turned to Fianna. She too was on her knees, leaning on one arm against the table. Her hair hung down along her face. Several bottles and tumblers had fallen from the table and lay strewn about the spread folds of her nightgown and wrapper.

"Goddamn you, Wallace," she said, her voice low and hard. She swept her hair from her face with one hand and sniffed. The movement caused her to lose her balance, and she had to grab the table again. "I told you there was nothing between us . . . *could never* be anything between us!"

Polk dropped his head even lower, then jerked it up, regarding her with crazy-bright eyes—the eyes of a dopehead, like those Prophet had seen in opium dens. Obviously, the druggist had been dipping into his own goodies behind the counter. "You goddamn bitch! You whore!"

"Shut up!"

Her scream on top of the gunshot still echoing in his head made Prophet's temples pound. Enough of this. He reached down, grabbed Polk under both arms, and heaved him to his feet, then shoved him out into the foyer.

"Goddamn her to hell!" the druggist wailed. Stumbling forward, he dropped to his knees, rolling up the runner around his shoes.

"Outside, Polk." Prophet jerked the man to his feet, then gave him another shove toward the front door. "Time to get sobered up, old son."

Polk turned to yell back toward the parlor, "You'll never get any more *gifts* from me, you goddamn, double-crossing bitch. Your father wanted you to marry *me*! That was his wish!"

"Shut up!" Fianna's voice broke on a sob.

Prophet turned the druggist around, shoved him through the inside door, across the porch, and out through the screen door. Polk stumbled down the brick steps and fell in the front yard.

He was making wheezing, grunting, crying sounds. Insane sounds. The sounds of a man so overcome with emotion he was like an animal.

Prophet hunkered down beside him, grabbed a fistful of the man's collar, and shook. Polk's head flopped back and forth. "You the bastard been taking potshots at me, Wallace? Huh? Are ya?"

He stared into the man's eyes. Polk stared back, glassy-eyed crazy, like some leashed stud dog heated up over some forbidden bitch two houses down. But for a moment, they acquired a genuinely befuddled cast, lines forming in the bridge of his nose.

He either didn't understand or didn't know what Prophet was talking about. Probably the latter. He'd just proven he wasn't much of a shot.

Prophet sighed and straightened. He had a mind to throw the druggist in jail with Leo Embry. But that wouldn't change anything that had happened here tonight. Polk wasn't a killer, just a hophead obsessed with a woman who didn't want him.

Glaring down at Polk, Prophet saw the wedding band on the man's finger. "Stay away from the lady," he ordered. "Whatever you had goin', or thought you had goin'—it's over. Go on home to your wife."

He turned, started back to the house, then stopped. Polk had leaned forward and was grinding his forehead into the grass, as though trying to burrow into the earth.

Prophet stared at him a moment, sucking his tooth. He really needed to get out of this town. "Polk, Polk . . ."

Polk looked up at him, tears streaming down his cheeks.

"You can pick your revolver up at the jailhouse tomorrow."

With that, Prophet turned to the house. As he did so, he saw two figures standing in the yard next door, silhouetted against the twilight sky. Neighbors. Behind the house, a dog was yipping. A horse whinnied in a pasture.

Prophet threw a neighborly hand out. "It's all right, folks. Just a little misunderstandin'." As he walked back into the house, he wondered how long it would take for this gossip to make the rounds.

The druggist, the bounty hunter, and the dead marshal's daughter . . .

He found Fianna where he'd left her, sobbing on the floor beside the table. He was about to kneel down beside her when he saw the cigar box next to her bourbon glass, on the smaller table beside her chair.

Curious, he went over and picked up the box, tipped it to the wan light filtering through a window.

Barely covering the bottom of the box was a fine, white powder. He knew what it was before poking a finger inside, then touching the powder to his tongue.

Cocaine.

One of Polk's "gifts," no doubt. Prophet had never indulged in the drug himself, but had been in enough opium dens across the West to recognize it.

A little made you sweet and dreamy. Too much turned your wolf loose. Fianna lay on the floor, knees beneath her, sobbing into her arms and crying, "Daddy, Daddy, don't leave me!"

She turned her head, saw Prophet holding the box and watching her with distaste.

"Give that to me," she sniffed, lifting her head and extending an arm. "Hand me the box."

"Nope." Prophet flipped the lid closed, set the box on the table, and crouched over Fianna, lifting her by the arms. "Time for bed."

He picked her up easily and, one arm under her neck, the other under her knees, carried her out of the parlor and into the foyer. "Okay," she said, regaining her saucy tone, "we can do that too."

"You need a long night's sleep. Then tomorrow should be a little better than today, and the next day better than that."

She tried kissing him, but he pulled his head away.

"Where's your bedroom?"

"Upstairs," she said through a sigh, wrapping her arms tightly around his neck and snuggling against him. "You feel nice."

"Don't do that," he said, breathing heavily as he climbed the stairs.

She nibbled his neck, feeling warm and soft in his arms. Her lips and teeth sucked and chewed at his neck, raising his temperature. "Can that shit," he growled. "Is this your room?"

She was too busy nuzzling his neck and licking his earlobes to answer him. Before him, a door stood ajar. He shouldered through it. In the dull light through the window, he saw a brass bed with a ruffled pink skirt, brushes, combs, and other female accoutrements strewn upon a dresser. On a small writing desk, books and papers were piled. The air smelled like her—lightly sweet nectar—minus the bourbon.

He laid her on the bed and tried to rise, but she kept her hands clasped around his neck. "No, don't go," she gasped. "Stay with me."

"Sorry, lady," he said, working her hands loose, "but I don't take advantage of liquored-up women."

"Oh, do!" She clung to him with a desperate, carnal

need that was almost palpable. Her breath was hot against his face. "Please stay. You won't regret it!"

She lifted her head, clamped her mouth over his, and thrust her tongue between his teeth. He tried to straighten, but she clung to him. He tried pushing her away, but the kiss and the musky warmth of her body against him drained the strength from his arms.

Stoked by hers, his own desire rose. He tried to fight it off, like an old lady chasing the same old neighborhood cur off her porch for the hundredth time in a year. But that cur would have none of it. It knew the old lady wasn't serious. She'd snarl and poke at him, but eventually she'd soften to his feeble yelps, warm to the charm in his eyes, put away the broom, and fetch him a bone.

That's what Prophet was doing now as he lowered himself and the girl back down to the bed—fetching his old, amorous, flea-bit mutt another bone, one of many he'd thrown it over the years. He kissed Fianna's cheeks, nuzzled her neck, smoothed her hair back from her face, and entangled his tongue with hers.

As he ran his big hands across her narrow shoulders, he removed the nightgown and the wrapper in one fell swoop, laying her out naked and pale before him—a long, willowy length of curving woman.

Her slender legs kicked as she begged him to take her. Her pale, almond-shaped breasts were exposed by the last of the day's feeble light washing through the room's single window, the nipples erect.

"Please," she whined, grappling with his cartridge belt, shoving at it, pulling, trying to get it off. "Take me!"

He heaved up on his knees, removed the belt, and dropped it to the floor. She was already pulling at the buttons of his denim jeans. He nudged her hands away, opened his jeans, slid them and his underwear down to his ankles. She reached for his member, ran her hands up and down its iron length, pressing it against her belly and sobbing, "Now!"

And then he was lying between her raised knees, propped on his arms, thrusting. She locked and unlocked her ankles around his back, pulled at his hair, clawed at his shirt, crying, "Harder! Harder!"

As he lay toiling between her knees, grunting, wheezing, and reeling, he knew he was making a big mistake. At any time, the man who'd been trying to ambush him could sneak into the house, or crazy Wallace Polk could return to finish the job he'd started.

This was the crazy kind of thing that got bounty hunters killed. Thinking with your pecker was a good way to get your head shot off.

But knowing that and being able to do anything about it were two different things. Prophet had made the same mistake before. But as he toiled and sweated atop Fianna Whitman's writhing body, feeling her skin stick to his, her mouth drawing wide and taut with every plunge of his body into hers, he knew he'd make it again.

And he'd continue to live as long as his luck held. When his luck ran out, he'd die. It was as simple as that.

But there were worse ways to go. . . .

He reflected on that as, ten minutes later, Fianna lay curled against him, sleeping with her head on his chest, one naked knee curled over his.

He'd pulled up his jeans, but he hadn't buttoned them yet. He would in a minute. But first he'd lie here, make sure she was fast asleep before he slipped away. He didn't want to wake her, but he also needed rest.

Yep, there were worse ways to go, all right. But now that his passion was spent, he lay here in the dark room, atop the quilts, listening for any strange sounds that might mean the drygulcher was near . . . or that Wallace Polk had returned.

The only sounds were two dogs barking desultorily and

a cow complaining in a pasture south of town. The house creaked when the breeze kicked up, fluttered the lace curtains out from the window. A wagon passed near the house, clattering over ruts.

The girl opened her mouth as she slept, and a thin trickle of drool puddled on Prophet's chest.

He stared at the ceiling, running the night through his head, trying to figure out what had driven Wallace Polk and Fianna Whitman to nose dope.

Prophet suspected that, in her case, it had something to do with her father, possibly about how he'd acquired his relative wealth as well as the grisly way he'd died. He might have been taking graft from saloon owners or confidence men, possibly whiskey traders, gunrunners, or rustlers. It was a common enough practice amongst poorly paid Western lawmen. If so, he and Fianna had been living on dirty money.

But what about Wallace Polk? What had rubbed his fur in the wrong direction?

Prophet wasn't finding anything out lying here—not that he really wanted to. He'd leave the town to its secrets once his reward money arrived and Henry Crumb returned.

And good riddance to Bitter Creek and its dunderheaded, drygulching townsfolk. . . .

Prophet slipped out from beneath the girl, covered her with a quilt, and dressed quietly in the dark room. A few minutes later, he stepped out the front door and stood in the yard before the porch. Gazing cautiously around the yard, he expected to see a gun blossom somewhere off in the darkness that had closed over the town.

After a quiet minute, he built and lit a quirley and headed back toward the main drag. He was nearly halfway there when he had a feeling he was being followed.

Twice he stopped, taking cover in the shadows of a chicken coop and under an outside staircase, watching and listening, smoking the quirley cupped in his left palm.

He saw nothing but the wind nudging shutters, a stray cat slinking behind an empty whiskey barrel, and Mad Mary coupling with some wheezing oldster in the alley behind the post office.

As he crossed Main, someone blew the glass out of the jailhouse only a foot right of his right shoulder. He hit the ground a second after the rifle's bark had reached his ears.

15

PROPHET ROLLED BEHIND the stock trough and clawed his Colt from his holster.

He peered over the trough's lip, casting his gaze across the street. Seeing no movement nearby—just the three dark hulks of the Main Street businesses directly across from the jailhouse—he looked to his right.

Nothing there but a few horses tethered to the hitch rack before the Mother Lode, the light gilding the worn ranch saddles. Two doors beyond the Mother Lode was the town's second saloon, the American. Smaller and with no whores or faro tables, it did less business. Still, three cow ponies and a buckboard were tied out front.

But there were no men in the street. No scudding shadows. No vagrant light winking off a rifle breech.

Prophet cursed. If the bastard wanted him dead so damn bad, why didn't he show himself and fight like a man?

Hoping to attract another shot that would give the shooter's position away, he leapt to his feet, stood still for a second, then bolted left and dropped to a knee, holding the revolver out before him.

Nothing.

Cursing like his grandfather used to curse at cotton-mouths in his fishing hole, he ran directly across the street. He pressed his back to the front wall of the women's millinery, looked around, and moved slowly to the building's west front corner.

He stole a look around the corner to the rear.

Seeing nothing but trash littering the sage between the millinery and the harness shop, he eased slowly back toward the rear. He was halfway there when a dark figure came around the rear corner, heading toward him.

Prophet's heart surged. He dropped to a knee. "Hold it there!"

The figure stopped and threw up his hands. "Don't shoot! Don't shoot!"

Prophet jogged toward him, Colt extended.

"Don't shoot!" the man repeated as Prophet approached. "I'm an innocent man!"

He was bulky and bearded, wearing a tattered bowler and a duck vest. An old, war-model Colt hung on his right hip. But there was no rifle. And Prophet's bushwhacker had definitely fired a rifle.

Prophet lowered his .45. "What the hell were you doin' back there?"

"You the new marshal? Oh, shit." His voice was deep and gravelly, as though he'd smoked cigars since he was ten. "Well . . . uh, I wouldn't want this gettin' back to my wife, but uh . . ."

"Come on!" Prophet urged. "Out with it!"

He jerked his thumb over his right shoulder. "You know, Mad Mary . . ."

"Ah," Prophet said dryly, remembering the oldster he'd seen wrestling with the whore a few minutes ago.

"I seen a man run back this way, though," the old man said. "Kinda interrupted me, if you know what I mean. And at my age, when you're interrupted, it ain't all that easy—"

"Which way'd he go?" Prophet shouted, peering into the darkness over the man's left shoulder.

"Straight back toward the windmill yonder."

Prophet ran that way, past a woodpile and the remains of one of the town's original tent shacks.

"Now, Marshal, don't go blabberin' about seein' me back here!" the old man called, his voice fading in the distance. "My wife wouldn't understand!"

Prophet ran along the south side of a post-and-rail corral, hearing the windmill clatter ahead. Approaching the windmill and stock tank, he slowed, swung his Colt from left to right. There wasn't much out here but a few widely spaced houses on brushy lots, a few small barns, corrals, and gardens amongst the rocky knobs and cedar clumps.

It was all cloaked in darkness, with no sign of the gunman.

Prophet walked to the other side of the stock tank and stared off into the ravine curving along the south edge of town. Nothing there either.

Once again, the man was gone.

Prophet brought his gaze in closer to his boots, hunkered down on his haunches, saw several fresh hoofprints. He studied the tracks by lighting several matches one after another, but saw nothing to distinguish the sign. No loose nails, splits, or shoe cracks.

He ran his sleeve across his mouth, stood, and holstered his pistol. He felt like raging into the darkness, daring the son of a bitch to get back here and fight like a man, but what good would it do?

Turning, he headed back toward Main, entered the jail-house, and fumbled around in the dark to light a lamp.

"What was that shootin' about?"

Prophet held the lamp high, casting the glow into the cell where Leo Embry stood, a few feet back from the door. The bandage on his head shown bone-white and rumpled against his youthful face with its grim eyes and smattering of red pimples around his mouth. His lips formed a sullen line.

"Bullet ricocheted off the wall and buzzed around in here like a bee." Leo's tone was indignant.

Prophet set the lamp down, grabbed the key ring from the desk, and opened the door. He had enough on his mind without having to worry about Leo Embry. Swinging the door wide, he stepped aside and said tiredly, "Get out of here, kid. If I see you in town again, I'm gonna cut your ears off."

When the kid just stood there, slow to comprehend, Prophet yelled, "Go on! Git! Get on back to where ya came from and stay there! You're no more a gunfighter than I'm a Baptist missionary."

The kid gave a surprised start, eyes snapping. "Y-you're gonna let me go?"

"Shake a leg before I change my mind."

Springing into motion but wincing painfully, Leo grabbed his hat off the cot and set it tenderly on his head. Leaving the cell, he sidestepped Prophet like a wounded bear, then made a beeline for the main door.

With one quick, skeptical glance over his shoulder, he turned right and disappeared, leaving the door standing wide open behind him.

Prophet shut the door and sat in Whitman's squeaky chair.

Who in the hell was trying to shoot him?

He doubted it was a professional. A short-trigger artist would have gotten in close and stayed there. Not taken a shot, then run with his tail between his legs. It was definitely someone good with a rifle, someone who lived around here. A stranger would stand out during the day. Another relative of someone Prophet had lately taken down?

No way to know till the man showed himself. Prophet just hoped he'd be alive to see the son of a bitch. What he needed at the moment, however, was a bellyful of vittles. The commotion had made him hungry.

He walked over to Gertrude's Good Food, where the cheery Frieda served him a fried steak with potatoes, a hot buttered roll, green beans, and several cups of tar-black coffee. She didn't do much flirting, what with several traveling salesmen at nearby tables, but her suggestive gaze held Prophet's several times, and she brushed her plump hip against his arm more than once.

He knew she wanted him to hang around for some more slap 'n' tickle, but he had too much on his mind. Besides, he'd done enough rolling in the hay for one day.

He was tired. Tired and weary and wanting to get shed of this town in the worst possible way.

Shouldering his shotgun and leaving Frieda a sizable tip from the two hundred dollars Crumb had left, like cheese in a trap, he left the café and walked back toward Main Street, where he checked both saloons. Quiet.

Wondering about the five gunmen he'd seen ride into town earlier, he headed for the whorehouse they'd visited. Hidden in the shadows east of the shabby, clapboard house unidentified by a sign, he watched a short black man in a knit cap leading the gang's five horses along the street, toward the stable in the backyard.

Inside, someone was playing a piano. The laughter of men and women trickled through the windows. Shadows moved behind the drawn shades.

It looked like the curly wolves were staying put for the night. That was all right with Prophet. He didn't want any more trouble. Hopefully, the gang was just passing through, and they'd mosey on down the trail first thing tomorrow morning.

He was in front of the jailhouse, halfway across Main, when he heard a sound. Hooves of a galloping horse thundered in the east.

Now what?

Turning, he squinted into the darkness until the form of a horse emerged. He drew his gun and watched a horse bear down on him, head down, hooves flying—a dark, fast-moving smudge against the starlit sky behind it.

Prophet was swinging his shotgun around to the front, but froze, staring. He couldn't see a rider on the horse's back. No saddle or bridle either. A loose horse.

Only, the horse was bearing down on him like a Nebraska tornado!

Prophet lowered the shotgun and bolted toward the jailhouse, at the last second diving from the charging horse's path. The horse had come so close to running him into the earth that Prophet could feel the *whush!* of the big animal displacing the air around him.

Prophet fell on his right shoulder, losing his hat, dropping the shotgun, and rolling. He lit on his heels and elbows, and turned, certain the horse had continued galloping westward along Main.

Nope.

The animal had skidded to a stop on its rear hooves. Digging its front hooves into the street's dirt and manure, it flattened its ears again, ringed its dark eyes with white, snorted loudly, and headed right back toward Prophet.

The devil's horse released from hell!

The bounty hunter got his boots beneath him and dove onto the jailhouse boardwalk, feeling the horse's right front hoof nick his foot as he went airborne. Ignoring the splinters digging into his palms, he rolled over to see the horse turn once again and lunge toward the boardwalk.

Prophet blinked, mouth agape. *"Mean?"*

He'd know that hammer head, those fight-shredded ears, and those crazy eyes anywhere, even in the dark.

Prophet scrambled aside as the line-back dun mounted the boardwalk, its hooves thundering and scraping over the planks. Mean and Ugly swung its head against Prophet, connecting soundly with the bounty hunter's left shoulder, sending him flying against the jailhouse.

The horse snorted and whinnied with glee.

"Mean, knock it off, you crazy bastard. You're gonna kill me!"

The horse snorted again. Prophet figured the next round would leave him battered into the logs and chinking of the old jailhouse, but the horse just stood there, nickering and jerking its head up and down.

Prophet chuckled. "Glad to see me, eh, Mean?"

Footsteps and labored breathing sounded westward up Main. "Goddamn horse!" cried a kid. "You okay, Marshal? I was leadin' the sumbitch over to the livery barn when he musta caught your scent and broke loose. He is yours, ain't he?"

"Yeah, he's mine," Prophet said, breathing hard and rubbing his sore shoulder, regarding the big line-back dun with both apprehension and pleasure. "Where in the hell'd he come from anyway? I left him in Cheyenne."

"Last stage just rolled into town about fifteen minutes ago. The driver had him tied on behind. He come with a note." The lanky youngster with a sharp chin and a billed hat fished a crumpled note from his pocket and handed it to Prophet. "Your tack's over to the livery barn. You want me to fetch it over here?"

"No, that's all right," Prophet said.

He tossed a quarter to the boy, who thanked him and headed back toward the stage depot. Behind him, Prophet uncrumpled the note and stepped into the street to read it by the light bleeding out from the Mother Lode. Mean and Ugly gave another snort and followed, staying close to Prophet's elbow, determined not to get separated from his master again.

Dear Lou,

You're the only one who seems to want this hammer-headed reprobate. The owner of the Federated Livery in Cheyenne was about to shoot him for fighting and tearing up stalls when I intervened and

*arranged for the stage line to send him on to you. I
hope you're still in Bitter Creek. What you see in this
animal, I do not know.*

*You owe me for the new hat he bit a hole in. I hope
this finds you well. I am heading toward the Southwest.
I hope I see you again before the snow flies. If not . . .*

> *I am, as always
> And forever shall be
> Yours, with love,
> Louisa*

Prophet smiled. He sniffed the note: licorice with a hint
of cherry sarsaparilla.

Louisa.

Slowly, thoughtfully, he folded the penciled notepaper,
stuffed it into his shirt pocket. Mean and Ugly was sniffing
and nibbling at the badge, which winked dully in the stray
light from the saloons.

"Yeah, I know," Prophet said, shoving away the horse's
long snout. "That tin looks as out of place on me as it
would on you. That's the straw I drew, but believe me, I'll
never get that drunk again."

He gave the horse a brusque hug, ran his hands down its
sweaty neck, pulled at its ears, and inspected it briefly,
making sure it had no cuts or deep bruises and that none of
its shoes had come loose. He drew a deep breath. The horse
smelled of sage and the night breeze . . . of crisp starlight
and the open trail . . .

Prophet stared at the horse and chewed his cheek,
thoughtful.

Finally, he picked up his shotgun, retrieved his rifle
from the jailhouse, locked the door, and headed west up
Main, toward the livery barn. Mean and Ugly followed
close on his heels, nickering playfully and nipping at
Prophet's shoulders and ears.

Prophet found his saddle just inside the livery barn's unlocked front doors. He quickly tacked up the horse, strapped his bedroll behind the saddle, shoved his Winchester into the leather boot, and mounted.

Mean jerked beneath him, muscles rippling. The horse kicked a back rear hoof out and gave a snort as Prophet reined him northward through an empty lot and heeled him into a canter. A few minutes later, they were riding through the rolling sage hills north of Bitter Creek.

A young coyote yipped to Prophet's right. A rabbit gave its befuddled shriek as a hawk or an owl nabbed it. The air smelled like cinnamon, sage, and cedar.

Prophet caught a fleeting whiff of some carcass rotting nearby—the remains of a coyote-killed deer, no doubt. Then the sage and juniper and dew-damp rocks took over again.

Prophet rode lightly in the saddle. Mean and Ugly stepped smartly beneath him, giving his hammer head an occasional energetic shake. His shod hooves rang off rocks, snapped limbs from low shrubs.

Horse and rider wanted to continue riding, but after he'd ridden a mile or so, Prophet turned back toward Bitter Creek. Reining up on a knoll, he studied the quiet town—a blue-black smudge in the starlight, with only a few shacks bleeding wan lemon light onto the sage.

Satisfied all was quiet, he made a cold camp in the hollow just north of the knoll, tied Mean and Ugly in high buffalo grass near a spring, and rolled up in his soogan.

He studied the stars for a long time, listened to the small night creatures burrowing into the grass and rocks and rotten logs. Mean and Ugly tore at the grass several yards away. The seep trickled tinnily, almost silently.

The coyote had ceased howling, but soon another started in, from a northern hogback, and then two more added their own refrains from the west.

Raucous yet melodic sounds, softened by distance.

Prophet slept.

16

PROPHET WOKE TO the scent of dewy sage tickling his nostrils, to meadowlark song, and to pale dawn light washing along the western horizon.

To the chittering of prairie dogs and raucous magpie chants.

To a giant muley buck padding toward him from the north, its big rack like an Indian's brush cage, its charcoal-crested neck and broad white chest ribbed with muscle.

The buck had come upon the camp from up breeze and, at once seeing and scenting human, it turned its head to gaze at Prophet askance through marble-black eyes. A second later, it twisted its heavy shoulders and trotted off through the brush, the thuds of its heavy hooves fading gradually.

Head turned on his saddle, hair mussed from sleep, Prophet watched the buck fade into the morning's blue shadows. He had no urge to reach for his Winchester. He killed only when he needed food, never for trophies. Trophy shooting was a low pursuit, fitting only for Eastern nabobs and Englishmen.

Mean and Ugly shook himself and nickered. The old familiar camp sounds caused Prophet's mouth to spread in a grin. The smile disappeared when he saw the tin star on his chest.

He had a job. Responsibilities. He had a long-headed fool out looking to let sunshine through his hide.

He tossed away the dew-damp blankets, got up, stretched, gave Mean a long, leisurely brushing, and saddled him. A few minutes later, he reluctantly mounted and turned the horse toward town.

The shadows were gradually lifting along Main when he rode in from the west. It wasn't yet seven, but several shopkeepers were sweeping dust and leaves from their boardwalks. Riding stiff-backed, Prophet searched the rooftops for the long, thin shadow of a rifle barrel canted in his direction.

Except for the industrious store proprietors and a few dogs heading home after their all-night country hunts, all was quiet.

At the east end of Main, Prophet turned toward Gertrude's Good Food. He pulled up at the hitch rack before the café, where a buggy and several saddle horses stood, then looped his reins over the rack, ordered Mean to behave himself, and went inside.

He took two steps and froze.

Sitting at a table to his right was the five-man gang of toughs who'd ridden into town yesterday afternoon. One of the men turned to him, raised an eyebrow, and cleared his throat. The others turned then as well.

They were a rough-hewn, gimlet-eyed lot, wearing the mustaches and long, brushed hair of professional gunmen.

"Mornin', Marshal," said the one nearest Prophet. His hair and beard were strawberry blond. His sun-bronzed cheeks were pocked and pitted. He stared at Prophet, faintly bemused, waiting.

"Mornin'," Prophet replied. No reason not to be sociable.

"Nice town you got here."

"Well, it ain't really mine. I'm only temporary. But thanks just the same."

The gunman's thin lips spread and the lids of his green eyes came halfway down. "The pleasure's all mine."

He held Prophet's gaze, and Prophet waited for him to say something else. The man's stare appeared at once forced and challenging, like he was daring an old dog to go for his ankle. After several seconds, the man turned to the others, nodded almost imperceptibly, and went back to his food. The others chewed down grins as they hunkered over their plates.

Puzzled, Prophet studied the gang another second, then headed for an empty table near two men wearing the worn suits and high-crowned hats of horse buyers, and sat down.

The girl Frieda employed to help with large breakfast crowds took Prophet's order and disappeared into the kitchen, where Frieda was cooking, knocking pans around and working the squeaky pump handle. Prophet tried not to stare at the gang across the room. He didn't want to provoke anything.

But who were they? What were they here for? How long were they staying?

He was half-finished with his own meal when the gang scraped their chairs back, stood, tossed coins onto the table, and moseyed toward the door. The cherry-blond who'd spoken to Prophet now turned to him again, grinned woodenly, pinched his hat brim, and headed outside.

Prophet only shrugged and kept his confounded muttering to himself. Those five were like pit dogs on short leashes. . . .

When he'd finished his own breakfast ten minutes later, he tossed down a dollar for the meal, added a tip, and stood. The waitress appeared at his side, her cheeks flushed from toil.

"Marshal, Miss Frieda would like you to stop by later

for dessert, after she closes for the afternoon. She said she had some legal matters to discuss."

Prophet stared at the waitress. He wondered for a moment if the girl was joshing, but her expression was serious. Then the kitchen door swung open. Frieda stuck her head out and stared at Prophet, eyes devilish, and winked.

"Oh . . . right," Prophet said, returning his gaze to the girl. "Tell Miss Frieda I'll try to make it back for, uh, dessert. . . ."

Behind the girl, Frieda's plump cheeks flushed as she smiled and withdrew into the kitchen.

"I'll tell her, Marshal," the waitress said and reached for his plate and coffee cup.

Prophet sniffed and adjusted his cartridge belt on his hips. A grass widow was a dangerous critter for a bachelor bounty hunter. . . . He pinched his hat brim to a couple of matronly ladies in the corner and headed for the door.

Outside, he mounted Mean and Ugly and reined back toward Main, straining his neck to look around for the drygulcher. A man couldn't let his guard down when someone was trying to turn him into a free lunch for the coyotes, and he was looking forward to catching the sumbitch and thrashing the holy hell out of him.

He rode up and down Main a few times, just to make his presence known, noticing several strange faces on the boardwalks—drifters, grub-liners, drummers. Fortunately, none looked like trouble.

He looked for Wallace Polk, curious about the man's demeanor the morning after he'd humiliated himself at Fianna Whitman's. Prophet hoped he didn't have another backshooter to worry about. While the drugstore was open and several ladies passed in and out, Polk himself was apparently staying back behind his counter, out of sight from the street.

Nursing one hell of a hangover, no doubt.

Prophet halted his horse at the east edge of town, just

beyond the frame brothel houses. He was about to circle around the town's north edge, hoping to spot a man with a rifle, when he saw the five gunslicks file out of the brothel they apparently were staying at. They set their hats carefully on their heads and kept to the south side of Main, heading west.

The shooters walked with long, confident strides. Several swept their frock coats back behind their pistol butts, making the weapons as visible as possible.

The two matronly ladies Prophet had seen in the café earlier stepped out of the millinery store, just ahead of the gunmen. The shooters paused, stepping aside to let the ladies pass, pinching their hat brims and smiling.

Seeing the gunmen, the ladies froze, eyebrows beetling. Chins up and lips pursed, they turned sharply, skirts, shawls, and hat feathers swirling, and crossed the street to the opposite boardwalk.

They continued walking east, shaking their heads and casting disdainful looks across their shoulders.

One of the gunmen waved. They all chuckled, continued strolling west to the Mother Lode, and disappeared through the saloon's swinging doors.

Prophet shook his head, scratched his ear, and scowled at the saloon's shuddering batwings. Those five were going to be trouble.

He just had a feeling. . . .

Early that evening, after a surprisingly uneventful day—aside from "dessert" with Miss Frieda, that is—Prophet's feeling was validated.

He'd just taken another ride around the town and was stabling Mean and Ugly, when a distant pistol shot sounded. It was muffled enough by buildings and distance that it could have been a branch snapping. But Prophet knew better.

Goosey after the several attempts to perforate his hide,

he immediately unsnapped the thong over his .45's hammer. Peacemaker in hand, he slung his shotgun over his neck and left the small stable flanking the jailhouse, walking around the jail to Main Street.

He stopped and cast his gaze up and down the near-dark street filled with the din of tinpanny music emanating from the two saloons.

The dozen horses tethered to the hitch racks before the Mother Lode were jerking around, startled. They tipped their heads back and pulled at their reins.

A man yelled something Prophet couldn't hear. The Mother Lode's piano fell silent. Another pistol shot cut the night's low din. A girl screamed. It was no scream of revelry. The girl was scared.

And it all seemed to be coming from the Mother Lode.

He'd just stepped into the street when another gunshot cracked. It was followed a half second later by the sound of shattering glass.

The horses were jerking around in earnest now, the saloon's bright lamplight bleeding through the plate-glass window to glisten along their rustling manes and saddles. When Prophet was about thirty feet from the saloon's big window, three men stepped through the batwings onto the boardwalk. Shaking their heads and muttering, they angled up the street toward the American.

As Prophet approached the batwings, the girl yelled once again. "What'd I just tell you, you little bitch?" retorted a man, his voice taut with anger. "And you," he said, "didn't I tell you to *play*?"

His brows beetled with wary wonderment, Prophet peered over the batwings. He could see little, however, for six or seven gents—cowpokes as well as a few businessmen—stood blocking the bounty hunter's view to the back of the room, where the trouble appeared to be occurring.

Prophet was about to step into the saloon when a big man standing left of the door turned to him. It was one of the five hardcases—taller than Prophet, with a slouch hat, spade beard, and light-blue devil's eyes.

His smile revealed both front teeth capped with gold. "Evenin', Marshal," he said coolly, in a faint Irish accent. "The boys're just lettin' their wolves run off their leashes a bit. Better run along and see if any dogs have treed any cats."

At the room's rear a man yelled, "No, goddamn ye . . . I *can't . . .* !"

There was more, but it was drowned out when the piano suddenly sprang to life with an overly energetic waltz. Prophet rose on his tiptoes to peer over the crowd, but the Irishman moved to block his view, his smile losing its luster. The big man shook his head and held out a big, freckled paw for Prophet's weaponry.

"If you wanna come in, you'll have to turn over the irons."

Prophet looked at him icily, anger tightening his jaw. Then he smiled and shrugged. "I reckon I'll find me a different party. Looks like fun, but thanks."

The Irishman smiled, the large, gold caps flashing in the gaslight emanating from the bracket lamps on both side of the doors.

When the bounty hunter had walked ten feet, he stopped and turned around. The Irishman had returned his attention to the show at the saloon's rear; Prophet could see only his grinning profile over the left batwing.

Quickly, hearing the girl crying beneath the clattering piano, Prophet turned left down the gap between the Mother Lode and the log shack housing a harness shop. He wended his way through the tumbleweeds and trash, took another left, and found himself looking up a set of stairs to the saloon's second story.

Hearing two more pistol shots followed by the girl's scream, he hurriedly climbed the stairs, clutching the shotgun before him, eyeing the door at the top of the stairs for possible trouble. The gunslicks might have posted a guard there too.

Finding the top landing clear, Prophet turned the door-knob and stepped quickly inside and right, pressing his back against the wall. A narrow hall opened before him, smelling musty and smoky. A single bracket lamp at the other end offered a weak, guttering light.

Men's laughter and a girl's cries rose from the first floor, along with the piano's frantic clatter and an occasional pistol crack. Prophet moved down the hall, holding the shotgun out before him, walking slowly but purposefully, chewing his cheek with concentration.

A few doors away from the door that probably led to the stairs leading to the saloon's first floor, Prophet paused. A girl was crying up here as well as down there.

"Don't hit me no more, Lars," the girl pleaded. "Please, I can't take it!"

"Shut up, goddamn your eyes!" the man called Lars yelled. A sharp crack, like that of a hard slap, rose from behind the door on Prophet's left. Lars laughed tightly. "Tonight, you listen to me, bitch! If I want you to cluck like a damn turkey, by God you'll *cluck*!"

He slapped her again.

Lips bunched with fury, Prophet swung the shotgun behind his back and unholstered his .45. Revolver in hand, he turned to the door, swung his leg back and forward, planting his right boot just below the knob. The door exploded inward with a crash, slamming against the wall as wood shards sprayed from the frame.

On the edge of the bed before him lay a naked girl, spread knees facing the opposite wall. A naked, soft-bellied man stood between her legs, facing Prophet over the width of the bed. He was poking the barrel of six-shooter into the girl's mouth, pinning her head to the mussed, bloody sheets.

The man snapped his head up at Prophet wide-eyed, face flushed with fury.

He yelled something incoherent as he jerked his re-volver toward Prophet, snapping off a shot that clipped the bounty hunter's collar before thumping into the wall be-hind him.

Coolly, Prophet raised his own revolver, fired, and watched the naked man stumble back from between the girl's spread legs, dropping his six-shooter and grabbing his chest with both hands.

Blood gushed through the man's hands as he pressed his back against the wall and, mouth drawn wide in a silent scream, sank slowly down to the floor.

Quickly, Prophet turned back into the hall and paused, listening. Another shot cracked below, and the piano con-tinued its crazy patter. There was a thumping sound, and the laughter of several men, the hoots and guffaws of sev-eral more.

Taking a deep breath, Prophet quickly replaced the spent shell in his Peacemaker and moved cautiously for-ward, heart pumping . . . well aware that all hell was about to break loose.

17

PROPHET OPENED THE door at the end of the hall and found himself on the balcony over the saloon. He turned right, crouched low, and moved to the rail, the piano's clatter now making his eardrums ache.

"Eeeee-*nowwwwwwwwwwww*!" a man screeched, clapping his hands. "Ride that horse, Janice. That's a girl!"

Spare chairs were stacked along the balcony's edge, offering cover. Through the chair legs and balcony rails, Prophet peered down through cigarette and gun smoke to the main floor.

His eyes slitted and his stomach did a somersault.

"Come on, Janice—hold on, girl!" a man's voice roared again, then admonished, "Keep movin', Burt. You stop, and I shoot off another finger!"

Directly beneath Prophet, within a semicircle of four seated gunmen, the saloon's owner, Burt Carr, was down on all fours, crawling around the floor. Janice, the blond whore with the heart-shaped face, was straddling his back.

She wore not a single stitch of clothes. She was crying

and clinging to the barman's collar, her pale knees pressed to his sides for support, her pear-shaped breasts swaying and bouncing.

Carr didn't look any happier than the girl. It was hard to tell from this distance, but he appeared to have lost a finger from his left hand, and the stump left a smeared path of blood on the floor as he crawled. The hardcases lounged back in their chairs, legs crossed, with cigarettes and soapy beer mugs in their fists. They laughed at the spectacle. They cheered, elbowed each other, pointed, slapped their thighs.

Thoroughly enjoying themselves.

Prophet's nostrils flared, and his chest burned with rage. The dogs indeed were off their leashes. . . .

Meanwhile, the ex-ranch cook and odd-job man, Sorley Kitchen, was playing the piano shoved up against the far right wall, his back to the room. His derby boasted two bullet holes in its crown, and there were two similar holes in the piano.

Kitchen ran his hands nervously over the keys, hitting as many sour notes as good ones while jerking nervous glances over his shoulder. Nervous sweat formed a broad, dark line down the back of his denim shirt.

Behind the semicircle of hooting gun toughs, several townsmen sat stiffly at their tables. Prophet saw the portly banker, Ralph Carmody, sitting with the lumberman, Milt Emory. Farther back, near the big front window, stood Wallace Polk, separate, alone, hands in his trouser pockets. His brown bowler was pulled low over his eyes as he worriedly chewed his cheek.

Several other townsmen stood about the room, observing the gunmen's bizarre festival with looks ranging from awful fascination to fearful repugnance. Behind them, the big Irishman stood guard at the batwings, grinning red-faced over the room, guarding his companions' backs.

"Come on, Burt—buck! I wanna see her titties jiggle!" ordered the man with the hard green eyes.

Prophet curled a nostril and grunted quietly through gritted teeth, "Now, that ain't sportin'."

The gang's leader extended a revolver over his boot resting on his knee, and fired. The piano player paused for half a second as the bullet drilled into the punchions near Carr's right knee.

The girl wailed.

The exhausted bartender, hair soaked with sweat, lifted his hands only about six inches before falling back to the floor, nearly collapsing as his elbows bent.

"Ah, come on, Burt!" the green-eyed gunman complained. "That ain't no buck!"

Casually, he thumbed the hammer back and extended the rifle over his boot, squinting down the barrel at the bartender's hand. Cursing under his breath, Prophet poked his Peacemaker through the railing and fired.

The slug smacked the extended gun with a metallic shriek, ripping it from the hand and tossing it halfway across the room, making several men duck from its path.

The gunman loosed a howl, grabbing his bullet-nicked hand and snapping his eyes up at Prophet. *"You . . . !"* he raged, spittle spraying from his lips, nostrils flaring.

"The rodeo's over," Prophet said, standing behind the rail, extending the Peacemaker in his right hand, the sawed-off shotgun in his left.

The hall had fallen silent. All eyes had turned to him, tense, waiting. . . .

It took about five seconds for the others in the hall to realize what had happened. The man to the green-eyed gunman's left made the first move, bolting to his feet and clawing his Beaumont-Adams revolver from his holster.

He had the pistol chest-high when his head took the blast from the sawed-off's left barrel. The distance was great enough, the spread of the buckshot wide enough, that the blast didn't blow the head off the man's shoulders, only turned it tomato-red and sprayed blood across the two men sitting on either side of him.

As the man stumbled backward, shrieking, his revolver popped, the wayward slug tearing into the green-eyed gunman's right boot toe, evoking another raucous bellow.

Now the three other gunmen, including the big Irishman by the batwings—had filled their hands with iron. Down on one knee, his face splattered with blood and wincing against the pain in his hand and toe, the green-eyed man shouted, "*Kill* that son of a bitch!"

Two pistols cracked, the slugs whistling past Prophet's head and burying themselves in the wall behind him.

Another gunman stepped behind a ceiling joist, his frock coat swirling about his holsters. He extended his revolver, fired two quick, errant shots, and ran for the stairs, taking three steps at a time as he headed for the balcony. Straightening from a crouch behind the railing, Prophet extended the barn-blaster straight out in his left hand, and fired.

"*Gee-awww!*" the man screamed as the double-aught buck took him through the chest and shoulders, blowing him back against the wall in mid-stride.

He bounced off the wall, dislodging a gaudy painting of a naked Indian girl riding a white horse. He stumbled forward and fell headfirst over the rail, somersaulting to the main floor.

He landed with a thud buried in the yelling and the pistol shots directed at Prophet, who'd dropped to his side, behind the railing, letting the slugs sail over him and into the wall or snap widgets from the scrolled rail supports. He cast aside the coach gun and extended the Peacemaker.

As a slug tore through a support post six inches to the right of his head, he fired two quick rounds. One clipped an empty chair while the other took the big Irishman, who was bolting around the tables holding a Winchester across his chest, through the shoulder.

The man cursed as the bullet spun him around and into a table, tossing the Winchester out before him.

As several more shots wracked the room, Prophet grabbed his shotgun and rolled back against the balcony's rear wall. Quickly, his hands working automatically, he broke open the shotgun and replaced the spent shells with new. Snapping the gun back together, he rose to a crouch, bolted forward ten feet, then ran to the railing.

As he extended the shotgun and thumbed back the rabbit-ear hammers, he saw that two tables had been over-turned. The fourth gunman and the green-eyed man, who'd produced another pistol, were hunkered down behind them.

To the table overturned on his left, he offered both bar-rels, the report sounding like a Napoleon cannon in the wood-lined room. The buckshot blew the table nearly in two, evoking pained cries from behind it. But Prophet didn't have time to survey his damage.

Dropping the empty shotgun, he crouched, ran back to his left, and extended the Peacemaker, thumbing back the hammer as the Irishman bolted out from behind a chair, yelling, "You're a dead son of a bitch now, me *boy!*"

He extended his own six-shooter, aiming toward the bal-cony. He and Prophet fired at the same time. The Irishman's shot nipped Prophet's left arm, just above the elbow. Prophet's shot crunched through the Irishman's brisket. Wailing and raging, flailing his arms for balance, the big man stumbled backward and crashed through an overturned table.

Spying movement to his right, Prophet turned to see one of the gunmen jerk Janice out from behind an overturned table in the room's southeast corner. "No!" she cried. She folded her arms protectively over her naked breasts and clutched her head. "Please don't shoot me! Stop!"

Burt Carr's head appeared above the table. He reached for the girl, but the gunman jerked her out of his grasp, thrusting her shieldlike out before him. Janice's face paint was smeared by perspiration and tears as she stared up at Prophet, beseeching.

Her light-blond hair hung in tangles along her face. Her pale, plump body looked terribly fragile against the tall gunman standing behind her, one arm crooked around her neck, the other holding a long-barreled Remington to her head.

Her lips trembled.

"Throw those irons down here," the man shouted through gritted teeth barely visible behind his soup-strainer mustache. "Or I drill daylight through this bitch's skull!"

Prophet straightened slowly, his pistol in one hand, the shotgun in the other, keeping them raised just above the balcony rail and extended only halfway.

"Now, why would you wanna go and do a thing like that?"

"I said—"

The crack of Prophet's revolver stopped the man only two words into his sentence, drilling a small, round hole through the left corner of his mustache. The man's head whipped back on his shoulders. Janice screamed and dropped to her knees as the Remington drilled a bullet into a rafter.

Prophet waited, Colt extended, to see if another shot would be necessary.

But then he saw the hardcase drop his Remington as he crumpled up beside the piano, near where Sorley Kitchen was cowering behind the overturned bench. The man panted like a dying dog, jerking both legs wildly.

Prophet slid his gaze through the smoke haze, looking around for more threats. What he saw resembled the aftermath of an Eastern hurricane. Tables and chairs were overturned, glass and bottles strewn about the floor, blood painting the sawdust, brass spittoons, square-hewn ceiling joists, and chairs.

Prophet caught only glimpses of patrons cowering behind overturned tables. One man had dived behind the bar; now he peered over the mahogany, only his scalp and eyes visible.

The only sound was Janice sobbing quietly where she had fallen onto her knees.

Three of the five gunslicks could be written off. The one Prophet had blasted from behind the table was questionable, hidden as he was beneath the rubble of the shotgun-blasted table.

The green-eyed man, lying under a broken chair, grunted and wheezed. Cursing, he flung the chair aside, heaved himself onto a knee, and grabbed a pistol off the floor. Grunting and wheezing, he climbed to his feet and hopped on one foot toward the batwings.

"Hold it," Prophet said, leveling his Peacemaker.

The man stopped, wobbled on his left foot, nearly fell, and turned, raising the revolver.

Wanting the man alive to answer questions, Prophet shot him through his left thigh. The hardcase screamed, fired a stray shot, twisted around, and dropped to both knees. Prophet hurried downstairs, keeping the Colt extended before him.

He was halfway across the room, kicking overturned chairs and tables out of his way, when the hardcase scooped the pistol off the floor. He turned toward Prophet, who stopped and said, "Don't do it, damnit!"

The hardcase grinned with savage defiance and extended his .44.

"Ah, shit," Prophet said.

He shot the man through the forehead, spraying the batwings with blood. The man flew onto his back, legs curled beneath his butt. His arms flopped like the wings of a wounded bird trying to take flight, then lay still.

Prophet lowered the Colt and walked to the gunslick, now staring up through his half-open, death-glazed eyes, the snarl still curling his mustache.

Blood dribbled down the batwings behind him, through which one of the saloon's disheveled customers slipped with a distasteful expression, and hurried off down the boardwalk.

Prophet looked around the room. Sorley Kitchen had crawled from his hiding spot and was bending over the hardcase lying under the table. The banker, Ralph Carmody, inspected the Irishman.

Prophet said, "He dead, Sorley?"

Kitchen nodded. "Just took his last breath."

Prophet turned to the banker. "What about yours, Carmody?"

"Deader'n hell." The banker gazed around the room, wincing and clearing the smoke from his face with his hand and regarding Prophet anxiously. "You killed 'em all, deader'n hell. . . ."

"Better them than me. Who were they anyway?"

Carmody glanced at Kitchen.

"Just owlhoots, I reckon," the banker said, avoiding Prophet's eyes. He looked at the five men who'd crawled out from behind their poker table near the front of the room. "One of you men fetch the undertaker, will you?"

As one of the five scrambled through the batwings, Carmody turned, looked around the blood and wreckage, grabbed his hat from under a chair, and headed for the batwings.

"Hey," Prophet called to the banker, wrinkling his brows. "Who were these men . . . and what in the hell were they doing here?"

Without turning, Carmody shrugged, paused before the doors, and wrinkled his nose at the blood. He jabbed the right batwing open with a finger, and slipped through the crack, careful not to spoil his fine, gray suit.

The other poker players regarded Prophet sheepishly

and, worrying their hat brims in their hands, headed for the door. "Frank, Shep," Prophet called to two of them, his voice raised with impatience, "who were these men?"

The two shrugged and filed outside.

Prophet turned to the back of the room. Several other customers had crawled out from their hiding places and were making for the door, avoiding Prophet's eyes.

Hearing a loud sob, Prophet turned to see Janice kneeling beside Burt Carr, wrapping the man's bloody hand with a handkerchief. As she worked, sobbing and sniffing, she seemed oblivious to the fact that she was as naked as the day she was born.

Carr's face was ashen and sweat-streaked, his lips stretched painfully back from his teeth. "That'll get me over to the doc, Janice. You . . . you best go on upstairs . . . take care of yourself. Take a bottle from behind the bar. On me . . ."

With another sob, she nodded, stood, and walked over to the bar, her full breasts jiggling. Her pale nakedness in the room's smoky ruins lent the room a dreamlike quality.

As she went behind the bar and removed a bottle from the back shelf, Carr headed for the batwings, squeezing his wounded left hand with his right. Then Janice walked up the stairs, the bottle in her hand, casting an oblique look at Prophet over her naked right shoulder.

When Janice disappeared through the door at the top of the stairs, Prophet and Sorley Kitchen were the only living men left in the place. Kitchen looked dumbly around for several seconds, slowly shaking his head. "Buckshot shore leaves an oozy corpse."

Seeing Prophet staring at him, scowling, he recoiled as if from a gunshot and bolted toward the entrance calling, "I'll help you over to the doc's place, Burt!"

Prophet stepped in front of the man, feet spread, blocking his way. "Old man, you ain't goin' nowhere till I get some answers."

The stove-up ranch cook was nearly bawling. "What makes ye think I know anything? I don't know *nothin'*!"

The old man was quicker than he looked; before Prophet could grab him, he'd feinted right and bolted left. When Prophet got turned around, all he saw were the two batwing doors shuddering in the oldster's wake.

18

HIS EYES FLINTY, Prophet turned back to the dead men.

He walked over to the leader, hunkered down on his haunches, and searched the man's pockets for identification, finding only playing cards, a derringer, and thirty dollars in silver.

He was patting down the man's vest pockets when he glanced at the sightless green eyes and froze.

There was something familiar about those eyes and soup-strainer mustache, that deep crease low on the left cheek. After a few seconds, a name washed up from the gloom.

Dean Lovell.

Regulator from Colorado and New Mexico. Worked for cattlemen mostly, but he wasn't picky—anyone who had a score they couldn't settle themselves. Prophet had seen him once before, with the famous cattleman Lou Dempsey in the Kansas House in Trinidad, Colorado.

Prophet left the silver and other possibles for the undertaker and headed over to Frieda's place for some answers he knew he wouldn't get anywhere else. Unless he put a gun to someone's head. He found the café empty. The lovely redhead was cleaning tables.

She looked up when Prophet walked in, slack with fatigue. "Lou!" Her eyes found the blood on his left arm and she added with quiet concern, "Your arm . . ."

He offered a wan smile. "Just a scratch." He sat down at one of the clean tables, setting the Richards on the chair to his right, tossing his hat down on top of it.

"I heard the shooting," she said, a sponge in her hand. "Vat happened?"

Prophet told her.

Silently, she turned, disappeared into the kitchen, and returned a minute later with two steaming coffee cups. When she'd set one cup in front of him and had sat down before the other one, looking distracted, he said, "Tell me what Lovell's doing here, and so help me, if you get a look like you just swallowed the whole hog—"

She looked at him hopefully. "You really don't know, Lou?"

"If I knew I wouldn't be askin' you."

"Crumb didn't tell you?"

"Didn't tell me *what*?"

"They vork for him. They're his—how do you say it?" She flexed her arm, until her right bicep bulged.

"Muscle?"

"Muscles. That's it."

"Muscle for what?"

She rose quickly, moved around the room pulling shades over the windows, and retook her seat across from him. Keeping her voice low, she said, "Mr. Crumb owns the town. All of . . . *us* . . . "

Prophet frowned. "What're you talkin' about—'owns'?"

"He owns all the land Bitter Creek vas built on. He bought it from the railroad for very little money, ven they decided not to run a line through here. But then prospectors discovered gold along the creek. People like my grandparents came here and bought land from him. The mining vas very big and the miners needed supplies and saloons and vomen and home-cooked food and . . ."

"I get the point," Prophet interrupted. "So they bought land from him and built their businesses. Then what happened?"

"The gold vent out. *Pinched* out."

"The miners left."

"Exactly."

Prophet sat heavily back in his chair. "Let me see if I got this right. You all paid *mucho dinero* for your land, assuming the boom would make you all rich. But the boom went bust, and now you're all stuck with land and property you can't pay for?"

"Vell, ve get traffic to and from the mines to the vest, and vith the business from the ranchers who've moved into the valley . . ." Her voice trailed off.

Prophet cocked his head and squinted one eye. "The boom busted, but you're still making money. What's the problem?"

She leaned over the table, her eyes wide, voice hard. "It's not enough to pay off Mr. Crumb's loans. Each month he takes half of our incomes to pay only the *interest* on loans ve couldn't pay off if ve had twenty lifetimes. 'Tributes,' he calls them."

"So let him foreclose, and get the hell out of here. You can all make fresh starts elsewhere."

"He von't foreclose. He von't let anyone who owes him money leave Bitter Creek. He owns the bank, everything . . . even several of the larger ranches."

"Well, hell," Prophet said, slamming his thumb down on a spoon, which flipped and rattled back down to the table. "He can't do that! It's illegal. Me an' Jeff Davis *lost* the war!"

Quietly, she said, "He has done it, Lou."

"With Whitman's help, I take it?"

"Yes."

"And Dean Lovell."

"Yes."

Prophet thought it over, frowning down at the spoon by his cup. "He paid Whitman a wagon load of money to make sure none of you slaves fled the farm, so to speak. But how did Lovell fit in?"

"Marshal Vitman vas just one man, and he vas old. Besides, he vas not as evil as Mr. Crumb needed, nor as capable. The Scanlons and the Thorson-Mahoney bunch vere proving too much trouble for him and his young deputy. So Mr. Crumb hired Lovell's gang to make frequent stops here, to spend a few days, to run off the troublemakers, and beat a few citizens to remind us all vat vould happen if ve didn't make our payments . . . or tried to leave."

Prophet chuckled at little Henry Crumb's enormous balls.

"It is not funny, Lou. People have died here, innocent people trying to flee. I have seen Mr. Crumb order men and even vomen vipped on Main Street."

Prophet stared across the table at her.

In a taut voice, she added, "Lovell vould spend a few days at a time here. Then he and his men vould leave, and ve could never be sure ven ve vould see them again." She paused. "But ve always saw them again."

Prophet laughed again, his eyes glinting darkly. "Shit."

She leaned toward him, a sorry smile pulling at the corners of her full mouth. "And now they are dead? *All* dead?"

"Deader'n hell. I'm glad I didn't know it was Dean Lovell. Mighta made me hesitate . . . and get ventilated."

Frieda threw her head back and laughed. She clapped her hands together once. "Lou, do you know vat this means?"

"It means Crumb's gonna be mad as a hornet when he gets home. 'Specially after I throw his fat ass in his own jail." A thought hit Prophet as he sipped his coffee. He set the cup back in its saucer. "What's Polk's part in this play-pretty?"

"You know about Mr. Polk?"

"Had a run-in with him over at Fianna Whitman's last night. He was in the saloon earlier, and I got the impression he wasn't too pleased about my airing out Lovell's hide."

Frieda bunched her lips angrily. "He is rat! A . . . stoolie bird . . ."

"Pigeon?"

"Yes, pigeon."

"How?"

"The only one who could pay off Crumb's loan. He comes from a vealthy family. He is . . . the vord is . . . remittance man. From England. Ven he paid off his loan, he bought in with Crumb . . . only he doesn't think anyone else in town knows."

Prophet just looked at her, waiting.

"He is Crumb's partner and acts as his stoolie pigeon," Frieda said. "He has job vere he sees many people every day, overhears our conversations. He spends every night in the saloons, eavesdropping on men for hints someone might be thinking about running away. It didn't take many killings and beatings before ve all got vise to who vas ratting the conspirators out."

"Neat."

"Ha! Yes, neat!" Frieda exclaimed.

"And with Crumb running the telegraph and controlling the stage depot, he'd know exactly what messages were going in and out and who sent them."

"Lou, do you know vy I am alone here? I am alone because Crumb killed my grandparents. Not directly, but the strain . . . and the vorry . . ."

"I'm sorry, Frieda."

She looked at him through tear-washed eyes. "And . . . and you are not going to help him. . . ."

"Did you really think I was?"

"No," she said, shaking her head. "But the others . . ."

"That's why all that silence in the saloon earlier," Prophet said. "They assumed I was in with Crumb and Polk."

Frieda scrubbed tears from her pink cheeks with a corner of her apron, sniffed, and smiled. Reaching across the table, she grabbed his hands in both of hers and said in a husky voice, "Lou, I am going to make love to you tonight . . . like no voman has ever made love to you before."

"Frieda, I shouldn't stay. I got a lot on my mind tonight, and I still have someone lookin' to turn me toe-down. . . ."

"Nonsense. You have given me my freedom, and I vill stay and I vill reward you vith my body."

Before he could respond, she'd bolted onto his lap and was squirming around on him and kissing him. His objections died in his throat.

A few minutes later, he found himself upstairs, slowly stripping the clothes from her deliciously fleshy body while caressing her breasts, pinching her nipples until she shuddered and gasped as she pushed him onto his back.

Breathing hard and grunting, she opened his pants, found what she was looking for, and went to work with all the thrilling magic she'd promised.

Frieda's ministrations quelled the gunfire in his head so that within an hour after they'd started frolicking in her squeaky bed, he felt as limp as a worn-out fiddle string. When they were finally through, Frieda doctored his arm and fell asleep on his chest.

He slept deeply, woke refreshed, and lay in bed going over the Bitter Creek situation in his head.

Finally, he dressed quietly so not to awaken Frieda, scanned the yard through the windows, and went outside. He was walking north along the trail toward Main fifty yards away, when a gun cracked and his hat was ripped from his head.

Damn. Didn't this fella ever rest?

Wheeling eastward, Prophet dropped to his belly and brought the barn-blaster up. A gun sparked fifty yards ahead, the slug kicking up gravel two feet before the bounty hunter's face. The shooter was too far away for the shotgun. Prophet unslung the lanyard from his shoulder, set the shotgun aside, and palmed his Colt.

The rifle cracked again.

Prophet fired two quick rounds at the gun flash on the shadowy prairie, waited, then fired two more. The shooter returned two shots from several yards left of where he'd originally shot from.

Prophet winced as one slug tore a branch off a shrub just ahead and right. The other slug whipped harmlessly over his head and spanged off a rock behind him.

Casting another glance along the prairie, he saw the shooter—a slender silhouette from this distance—retreat toward the northeast, running. Prophet muttered an oath, bolted to his feet, and gave chase, leaping over fallen mesquite branches, rabbit brush, and sage tufts.

When he saw the shadow stop, he leapt to his right, rolling off a shoulder and coming up to see two muzzle flashes. He emptied his own pistol at the purple dot moving against the milky eastern horizon.

He'd run fifty yards when he lost the dot.

He continued running, but stopped suddenly when the shooter bounded up from a swale on a piebald horse, making a hard, fast beeline toward Prophet, the hooves pounding, the horse blowing, the rider hunkered low over the animal's neck and yelling, "Gid-up, goddamn ye. Gid-up now . . . go . . . !"

Prophet brought up his Colt and thumbed back the hammer. Remembering he'd fired his last round, he cursed, dropped the revolver back into its holster, turned toward the oncoming horse, and crouched defensively.

The rider clawed his own revolver from the holster on his right hip. Prophet dove left as the man fired three errant rounds. When the man was thirty feet away, he again raised the revolver and fired, but the jouncing saddle threw off his aim, and the slugs plunked harmlessly into the turf.

Prophet flung himself behind a rabbit bush, and the man's last two shots whistled over his head. The bounty hunter peered over the shrub. The horseman checked down his piebald only ten feet away. Cursing, the man neck-reined into a retreating turn.

Prophet bolted out from behind the shrub and threw himself against the horse, clawing at the shoulder of the gunman's long denim coat.

Doing so, he looked up into the square, fair-skinned face, thin lips twisted into a snarl, the deep-set eyes hooded with exasperation.

Prophet's hand slid off the man's shoulder. The rider jabbed an elbow hard against the bounty hunter's forehead, igniting sparks behind Prophet's eyes.

For a moment, the world dimmed, and then the bounty hunter felt himself rolling over the sagebrush and low rocks as he watched the rider angle away. The gunman spurred the piebald savagely. The horse dug its rear hooves into the prairie, whinnied, and galloped west.

"I'll be back, ye son of a bitch!" the fair-faced gunman yelled over his bobbing left shoulder.

Prophet rose onto his knee. Catching his breath, he gritted his teeth and watched the drygulcher merge with the northern hogbacks.

"No, you won't, fella," Prophet wheezed between breaths. He heaved himself to his feet and took mute inventory of his minor aches and pains. Still staring after the rider, he brushed the dirt from his torn denims. "I'm after you now."

19

PROPHET RETRIEVED HIS hat and the .45 that had fallen from his holster when he'd jumped at the gunman, and saddled Mean and Ugly. A quarter hour after the attack, he was following the gunman's trail through the hogbacks north of Bitter Creek, the roofs of which the sun slowly gilded behind him.

A mile north of town, the drygulcher had followed a small creek, then turned up a steep hill through scattered aspens and pines. Following the sign, Prophet crossed two ridges, rising deeper into the mountains. By the time the sun had climbed halfway up the eastern sky, he reached an obscure canyon where the gunman had picked up an old mining road.

Ten minutes later, Prophet came to a clearing where a sorry-looking tangle of peeled-log corrals huddled close to a shack fronting a mining portal cut into the high canyon wall. Prophet slipped out of the saddle and tethered Mean in a natural trough. Holding the Richards in his right hand, he crept to the floor of the canyon and hunkered down behind a boulder sheathed in shrubs.

The sun had found the canyon and was gaining strength

even at this altitude. Chipmunks prattled from overarching limbs. Prophet scrubbed sweat from his brow and stared across the piñon-studded canyon floor at the cabin.

Smoke curled from a tin chimney pipe. A piebald and a blue roan milled in the corrals, a saddle draped over the top slat, near the gate.

Prophet studied the cabin for a long time, watching and listening with his hawk's eyes and ears. He was wary. The man had to know Prophet could track him here. The son of a bitch could be waiting with a rifle.

Prophet scrubbed his jaw with his left hand, considering making his way to the cabin's rear. The front door opened. The man appeared in a blue shirt and long denim coat, cartridge belt and holster buckled around his waist.

Prophet's eyes narrowed. A short bulldog with close-cropped sandy hair and long sideburns headed for the gray-board privy off to the right and went inside.

Prophet hunkered down, watching, feeling the adrenaline spurt. The man was either trying to bait Prophet into a trap, or he was suicidally stupid. Based on the man's previous ineptness, he was probably stupid.

Prophet bolted out from behind the boulder and ran across the canyon floor, crouching and weaving between shrubs, keeping an eye peeled on the cabin for other shooters. Nearing the privy, he ran on the balls of his feet, stopped before the door, and raised the Richards.

A single, explosive blast of double-aught buck blew away the locking nail and put a hole big as a wheel hub where the knob used to be. Prophet stuck his left hand through the hole and gave the door a yank.

It flew back and Prophet bounded forward, short-barreled barn blaster extended in his right hand.

"Mother of Christ!" yelled the bulldog, sitting on the privy's single hole, jeans and summer underwear bunched around his boots. He reached across himself for the Colt Navy to his left.

"Want the other barrel?" Prophet asked him.

The man gulped as he stared fearfully down the Richards's yawning maws.

"Who are you?" Prophet asked.

The man didn't say anything.

Prophet thrust the Richards to within six inches of the bulldog's face. The man recoiled against the privy's back wall, nudging a small calendar hanging from a nail, and turned his head to one side, blinking fearfully, awaiting the blast.

"Wales," he screamed. "I'm Edgar Wales! Please don't shoot me. My momma's back in Denver . . . and I send her money."

"Why are you potting for me, Edgar Wales?"

Prophet thumbed back the Richards's right trigger and snugged the barrel up to Wales's jaw. "Looks like your momma's gonna be diddlin' drifters for Colfax Avenue pimps."

"Ralph Carmody hired me!" Wales yelled, adding in a softer voice, "And . . . and several other businessmen from Bitter Creek."

Prophet's blood warmed. "Why?"

When the man just grunted and pressed his head to the privy's rear wall, wincing, Prophet poked the barrel hard against his jaw. *"Why?"*

"Oh, Lordy," Wales whined, squeezing his eyes shut and panting. "'C-cause they think you throwed in with Crumb. They want you outta the way so's . . . so's I can ambush Crumb and his new marshal when they ride back to town . . . Oh, Lordy, please don't shoot me. I just work for Mr. Boggs out to the Lazy Z. I'm a good shot with a long gun, but I ain't no *real* killer! I reckon I'm as good as they could find since Carmody's grandson refused to do it, but I'm just a plain ole thirty-an'-found cow waddie!"

He turned his head. His eyes widened, surprised to see that Prophet had withdrawn the shotgun.

"Stand and pull your pants up."

Wales studied Prophet skeptically. "Wh-what you gonna do?"

"Haven't figured that out yet. Get up."

Awkwardly, keeping his eyes on the Richards, Wales stood and pulled up his pants, tucking in his shirt. When he'd buttoned his fly, he reached for his pistol belt.

"Leave it," Prophet said. "Get those hands raised."

Wales sighed with chagrin and raised his hands. Prophet backed up and turned. Still watching the barn-blaster extended from Prophet's waist, Wales stepped out of the privy.

"The corral—move," Prophet said, waving the shotgun toward the horses.

"Listen, mister," Wales said. "I was just doin' what I was told . . . what they paid me for. Me, I mind my own business mostly, herd cattle for Mr. Boggs. I don't—"

Wales jerked around, grabbed Prophet's shotgun barrel in both hands.

Prophet didn't even have time to shout a warning.

Wales gave the blaster a jerk. The sudden, violent movement thrust Prophet's finger against the right trigger. Instantly, the Richards bucked.

The shotgun's explosion was partially muffled by Wales's belly. The single barrel of double-aught buck lifted Wales straight up off the ground and back about six feet.

He hit the turf on his back, offering a strangled cry, hands feeling for his guts, which were no longer there but had been blown through his spine and deposited on the sage and sand behind him.

Wales kicked his legs, bending his knees against the pain. He stared up at the sky and moved his lips as though trying to speak, lifting one hand, waving one finger as though there were one more thing he wanted to say.

Prophet crouched over him, hands on his knees. Wales's deep-sunk blue eyes rolled around in their sockets, turning glassy. "What's your momma's name?" Prophet said. "I'll write her, tell her what happened."

Wales's eyes fluttered. "I don't ... have no ... momma," he rasped, blood welling up from his chest and throat and dribbling down his chin. "Never did have ... none."

His head turned to the side. His chest fell and did not rise again. His feet jerked, and then he lay still.

Prophet straightened. "Dumb bastard."

Feeling bad about taking down the cow waddie, he broke the Richards open, extracted the two spent shells, and replaced them with fresh ones. He glanced down at the dead man again.

"Dumb bastard," he repeated. He looked around the cabin, then slung the Richards across his back and tramped over to the corral.

A quarter hour later, he'd tied Wales to the back of the dead man's horse and was leading him back to Bitter Creek, Mean and Ugly fidgeting at the smell of blood. "Come on, Mean," Prophet cajoled as they turned south onto the old mining road. He was in no mood for the horse's melodrama. "It ain't like you never smelled blood before."

In town, Prophet inquired at the bank for Carmody, then rode over to the Mother Lode. He tied Mean to the hitch rack, cut Wales's blanket-draped body free from its rawhide ties, and slung the cadaver over his shoulder.

He pushed through the batwings and looked around the dim tavern. Burt Carr was swabbing the bar with his left hand, the bandaged right hanging at his side.

Janice lounged against the bar in a crimson dress, black feathers in her hair, a matching bruise sheathing her left eye. Both turned to watch Prophet, as did Sorley Kitchen, hunkered over a beer at the other end of the mahogany.

Seeing Carmody, Prophet crossed to the table around which the banker and several other businessmen were taking a beer and poker break, cigars smoldering in ashtrays. Prophet paused before the table.

The men looked up at him and seemed startled.

"What the . . . ?" Milt Emory drawled around the cheroot in his teeth.

Prophet bent his knees slightly and gave the body a heave. It hit the table with a crash, cards scattering, beer mugs hitting the floor and shattering. The blanket fell from Wales's body, revealing the glazed eyes and gaping, ragged wound. Blood smeared the table.

Carmody leapt from his chair, a fan of cards in one hand, a cigar in the other, a scowl on his red face. "What's the meaning of this?" he bellowed, shuttling his exasperated gaze to the dead man. The banker's jaw dropped.

"Your assassin done got his lights blown out . . . not to mention his guts," Prophet said.

Carmody's eyes grew wary.

"I'm not on Crumb's side, you wooden-headed shoat," Prophet said. "You got this dumb bastard cored for nothin'."

Face creased with disgust, he turned and was walking toward the door when Carmody said, "What about the reward money?"

Prophet turned back, frowning. "What reward money?"

"The money the express company wired here. Crumb said he was holding it for you. It's in my vault." Carmody glanced at the other businessmen, who looked confused. "I thought you'd bought in with Crumb. . . ."

"Like Polk," Emory said.

Prophet stared at the men and scratched his ear. His money had come in. Crumb had duped him into staying.

In spite of himself, he chuckled, plucked a previously rolled quirley from his shirt pocket, stuck it between his teeth, and grabbed Carmody's cigar.

He glowered at each man in turn as he touched the cigar to his quirley. Puffing smoke from the side of his mouth, he tossed the cigar back to the banker, who fumbled with it, brushing hot ash from his suit.

"If I had any brains," Prophet said, "I'd ride out of here and keep on ridin'. But my ma always said I didn't have the good sense I was born with, so I reckon I'm gonna stay long enough to throw Crumb and Polk in their own jail. What happens to Bitter Creek after that is up to you."

Quirley smoldering between his teeth, Prophet turned and pushed through the batwings. He walked across the street, scaled the raised boardwalk before POLK'S HEALTH TONIC AND DRUG EMPORIUM in a single bound, turned the doorknob, and frowned.

Locked.

He backed up and peered in a window.

"He didn't open today," said an elderly, heavy-set woman passing on the boardwalk behind him.

Prophet stood back and peered at the building, puffing the quirley in his teeth with consternation. "Well, I'll be—"

A shrill scream rose in the south. It died only to rise again, so horror-pitched that it pricked the hair on the back of Prophet's neck and ran chills up and down his spine.

Letting the quirley drop from his teeth, he turned around, grabbed his Colt, and ran. Boots pounding, he lurched past the Mother Lode and jogged down the space between buildings.

The scream rose again, trilling throatily. Homing in on it, Prophet dashed through a yard, scattering chickens and startling two horses in an open stable. Behind a board shack, a tall, skinny man in coveralls stood peering south.

Prophet stopped and followed the tall man's gaze.

Mad Mary cowered in the yard before the Whitman house, about fifteen feet from the front porch. Suddenly, her head rose and her mouth drew wide. She loosed a scream like a Blackfoot witch conjuring evil Sioux-bedeviling spirits.

Prophet walked slowly toward her, gazing around, seeing nothing but the surrounding shacks, privies, stables, and a few neighbors who'd been drawn by the screams. Hearing the squawk of a screen door, he raised his eyes to the Whitman porch.

The screen door opened slowly.

Fianna Whitman stepped onto the porch in a dark blue dress with white lace around the collar and sleeves, her hair pulled back in a bun. Holding her stomach with her right hand, she moved stiffly forward and slowly descended the steps.

She faltered, grabbed an awning post, teetered as though buffeted by a stiff breeze, then sank slowly down to the steps.

Prophet ran into the Whitman yard.

"Fianna?" He crouched down beside her, saw the blood matting her left breast.

Her eyes were soft and rheumy from shock.

Prophet turned to the men trailing over from the saloon, drawn by Mary's screams, and yelled, "Get the doctor!" He turned to Fianna and, his voice low, asked, "What happened? Who did this?"

Her eyes narrowed briefly, as though against a sudden pain spasm. "Wallace," she said just above a whisper. "He couldn't get it through his thick head that we . . . never. . . " She swallowed, panting. "Lou, he's gone to warn Crumb."

She winced. Sweat beaded her forehead, pasting her hair to her cheeks. Then the pain spasm passed, and her eyes found Prophet's again, her full lips quirking another half smile. "Lou?"

Prophet slipped his right arm behind her head, cushioning it from the step. He slid up close beside her, to keep her warm. Blood oozed from her left breast.

"Shhh. Doc's on the way."

"Thanks . . . for the other night."

He beat away a bitter frown with a smile. "My pleasure."

"I didn't deserve such sweetness."

She smiled balefully and winced. Her eyes rolled up, and the light left them. The lids drooped. Her head canted against his shoulder.

Tenderly, Prophet smoothed the hair back from her cheek. Someone moved up on his left, and he turned to see Ralph Carmody approaching, his features drawn, his hat in his hands. The others from the saloon stood at the edge of the yard, not knowing what to do.

"What happened?"

"Polk," Prophet said.

Carmody shook his head, befuddled. "You seen him?"

"No, but Mary must've seen it all. Miss Whitman told me she offered her food and the bed in her back room from time to time."

Prophet slipped out from beneath Fianna and walked over to Mary. He crouched, grasped the withered woman's shoulders in his hands, and shook her gently.

"Polk," Prophet said. "Which way did he go?"

Mary sobbed, lifted her head as if to scream, then closed her mouth and extended her right arm west.

Prophet released her, straightened, and tramped through the scattered crowd toward Main Street.

"Proph, can I ride with you?" It was Ronnie Williams running up beside him.

The kid knew this country better than Prophet did.

"Get your horse."

20

IT WASN'T HARD to cut the relatively fresh sign of Wallace Polk's galloping horse from the wheel ruts along the mining and mail road leading west from Bitter Creek.

As Prophet and Ronnie alternately loped and walked their horses through the sage-tufted hogbacks and sandy rimrocks, Prophet hoped to gain sight of Polk before dark, about four hours distant, and let the druggist lead Prophet to Crumb and Crumb's new "lawman"—all of whom he hoped to throw in the Bitter Creek jailhouse.

But he'd not hesitate to kill if it came to that. Crumb and Polk were two of the most cowardly killers he'd ever known.

It was a good plan, and it should have worked.

Only, Prophet didn't count on Polk being able to stay ahead of him until dark. The druggist, probably knowing Prophet would be trailing him, and taking the livery's fastest horse, had done just that.

The sun was a bright, bloody blossom behind the dark western peaks when Prophet and Ronnie stood on a low butte, their horses' reins in their hands, a sage-spiced breeze wafting against their faces. Prophet stared dully southwest, knowing he could ride no farther without risking losing Polk's trail in the darkness.

He and Ronnie would have to bivouac for the night and begin following Polk's sign again in the morning.

They made a cold camp, saying little. Lying in his blanket roll, Prophet watched in his mind's eye as Fianna Whitman walked out of her house again, hand across her stomach, and slouched down to her porch steps. He thought of Frieda. He'd had to leave town without telling her the reason; when she didn't see him tonight, she'd wonder.

He and Ronnie were in the saddle again as soon as the dawn showed them Polk's hoofprints traversing an old trapper's trail known as the Medicine Bow cutoff.

"Crumb must've met his lawman fella somewhere around Broken Lance," Ronnie said as they trotted their horses through a pine forest, chickadees chirping in the branches. "Must've come up from western Colorado."

"I wonder if it's Grant Schaeffer," Prophet said.

"Who's he?"

"Lawman and hired gun. Shirttail relative of Wes Hardin. They call him the Eagle 'cause he's got the glassiest pale blue eyes, and they say he can shoot a spider off a fence post from a hundred yards. He wore a badge in Deadwood and Leadville, then got caught rigging faro games and selling hooch to Injuns. Last I heard he was in Utah. He's the only man of his ilk I can think of who Crumb might've found out this way. Bitter Creek would be a fine remote place for the Eagle to hide out a few years . . . and make some money in the process."

Prophet turned to Ronnie, who flinched under his dark gaze.

"If it's him, you stay clear. Been enough folks killed in Bitter Creek without the ole Eagle addin' you to the boneyard."

Late that afternoon, they found a cold fire pit in a narrow mountain valley, where Polk had met up with two riders who'd ridden in from the southwest, Crumb on his way back from wherever he'd picked up the new marshal of Bitter Creek.

"Why didn't we meet 'em on the trail?" Ronnie asked, looking around the fire ring at the cropped grass where three horses had been picketed last night.

Prophet was walking west through the brush, eyes on the ground.

He walked several yards away from the fire ring, lifted his head, and peered straight west. Finally, he threw out an arm and said without turning, "Looks like they headed through that gap in those hills yonder."

"Trying to get around us?"

Prophet slowly shook his head. Scowling, he tramped back to the fire ring, grabbed Mean's reins, and climbed into the saddle. "We'll see. Keep your eyes peeled. Polk's told 'em the whole story by now, and they might try to bushwhack us."

They followed the gap through the sunburnt hills, and rode for a good hour through rolling sagebrush and high, craggy rimrocks. The trail of Polk and the other two men followed a creek, which Ronnie told Prophet was the Jackrabbit, feeding the Sweetwater up near the Buffalo Buttes. They spotted a few rangy cows on the hillsides and occasional dry pies littered the stream bank.

"It's been a while since I rode out this far from town, but I'm pretty sure we're on Jackrabbit range," Ronnie said, eyeing one such cluster of cow pies.

"What's that mean?"

"It means we're in trouble," Ronnie said, cutting his eyes around. "The Jackrabbit's run by Jedediah Spillane. He's business partners with Crumb; Spillane's half owner of both Bitter Creek saloons and both brothels."

"So Crumb's headin' for the Jackrabbit for help." He

paused, thinking it over. Polk had found Crumb and the gunman, told them how Prophet had wiped out the Lovell bunch, so they'd headed for the Spillane spread to recruit a few of the rancher's best shooters.

"How many men does this Spillane have on his roll, Ronnie?"

The kid shrugged. "It ain't a real big spread, and I heard since Spillane's old, he ain't been adding to it. I'd guess no more than ten. But most of 'em are fightin' men."

"This far off the beaten path, and in Ute and Cheyenne country, they probably have to be."

Prophet looked around, made sure his pistol and shotgun were loaded, then snugged his hat down and kneed Mean into a trot.

Late afternoon found them dismounted and lying prone behind the lip of a high ridge, their horses ground-hitched at the base of the butte behind them. Keeping his head low to the grassy lip, Prophet stared through his field glasses at the ranch headquarters nestled in the brushy hollow below.

The compound consisted of a weathered, L-shaped cabin, two hay barns, several corrals, a windmill, and a simple log bunkhouse beside a blacksmith shop. Horses milled in the corrals, and several men were working the rough-string broncs near a snubbing post.

The mustachioed Mexican blacksmith hammered the hub of a big Murphy hay wagon while two collie dogs sat behind him, staring at the black-and-white cat cowering at the edge of the shop roof, tail curled over its back. The dogs wagged their own tails and eagerly shifted their front paws.

Prophet focused on the main house, before which three horses were tethered to a hitch rack. Two drank water from a stock trough. The third lowered its head and shook itself, making the stirrups of its saddle flap like wings. The coats of all three horses shone with sweat.

Prophet lowered the glasses and turned to Ronnie. "That's what they've done, all right. They've gone for help."

Ronnie squeezed his rifle tensely. "What now?"

Prophet scanned the ranch again. Finally, he lowered the glasses and turned to Ronnie. "Is there a direct trail between here and Bitter Creek?"

"The Mud Creek Trail is about as direct as it gets out here."

"Would they take it?"

"I don't see why not."

Prophet spit. "We head up trail a ways, hunker down, and wait for Crumb, Polk, and whoever else to head for Bitter Creek."

He and young Ronnie crawled backward down the hill then, well below the ridgeline, stood, and jogged down the grade to the horses.

They mounted and rode through rough country cut by draws and dry creek beds, seeing more cattle but twice as many black-tail deer and one rare black coyote with a white-tipped tail. Some Indian tribes regarded a brush with such a beast as bad luck; others had determined it good. Riding out here in Indian country, with a gunfight with white badmen imminent and only one man to back his play, Prophet silently prayed the coyote meant Crumb and Polk's asses would both belong to him by this time tomorrow, and not the other way around.

Prophet wanted to intercept Crumb and Polk far enough away from the ranch that their gunfire could not be heard at the Jackrabbit headquarters. Near dark and after another hour's ride, he and Ronnie hunkered on a slope strewn with rocks and boulders and stipled with wind-twisted pines. The trail cut through the narrow pass fifty feet below, a pale ribbon between steep, jagged walls.

Taking positions on either side of the trail, they waited through the long, starry night, watching and listening. They waited through the morning and early afternoon. Prophet was beginning to think Crumb had chosen a different route back to Bitter Creek when he spied movement south and west along the Mud Creek Trail, a half mile before the pass.

He raised his glasses, brought the seven riders into focus.

Henry Crumb, in his gray suit and bowler hat, rode at the head of the pack, beside a man dressed in a tailored dark suit with a high-crowned tan hat with a Texas crease. The man was as slightly built as Crumb, but square-shouldered, and his face looked slapped together from plaster, with a dark, buckhorn mustache waxed and curled high at the ends.

He rode stiff-backed and forward, butt lightly slapping the saddle. Holding his reins high and close to his chest, he stared intently over his black's bobbing head—resembling for all the world a human hound scenting blood.

Prophet chewed his lower lip and chuffed. Grant "The Eagle" Schaeffer. The new marshal of Bitter Creek.

He glassed the others in the pack, saw four men dressed in drovers' garb, six-shooters on their hips, rifles in their saddle scabbards. Deciding the four Jackrabbit riders were nothing special, just fair-to-middling firepower whose purpose was merely to back the Eagle's play, he raised the glasses a notch.

Polk rode at the tail end of the pack, not looking quite so mild-faced today.

Anxiety creased his eyes as he slouched in the saddle, elbows rising high with his mount's every lunge, his dusty dress coat flapping out behind him, the brim of his derby pasted against his high forehead. Several times he shook his head as if to clear it, and lowered his head to brush his nose against his right arm, once nearly losing his hat in the process.

"You and Crumb are at the end of your run, Wallace," Prophet snarled as he glassed the man, who suddenly grabbed his saddle horn to keep from falling. Prophet snorted. "In spite o' your nose candy, you know it."

Prophet lowered the glasses, turned to where Ronnie hid in the rocks on the other side of the narrow defile, and raised his right arm. The kid waved. Grasping his Sharps in both hands, he doffed his hat and hunkered low between two boulders.

Prophet waited until the riders were within fifty yards, then scurried out from his rocky niche, leaping onto a flat-topped boulder below. He stood there, boots spread, his rifle held low across his thighs.

Absently, he chewed the quirley in the right corner of his mouth, staring, waiting.

Only a few seconds passed before Schaeffer spotted him, the gunman's chin raising, his body tensing. The man held up a gloved hand; with the other he reined his horse to a halt.

The others checked their own mounts down and turned to the gunman curiously, several murmuring questions. Schaeffer replied by extending his right arm toward Prophet.

The others tensed, holding their reins tight in their gloved hands. Several shucked rifles from their saddle boots or revolvers from their cartridge belts. Crumb grabbed his own six-shooter and held the barrel in the air while staring toward Prophet, his horse prancing nervously beneath him.

Prophet glowered at the group through the rising dust, working the quirley from one corner of his mouth to the other. The riders were about thirty yards away and tightly bunched, well within rifle range.

When the group's collective murmur had died and the horses had settled down, Prophet called, "Crumb, Polk, your trail ends here!"

The group just stared at him. Finally, Crumb glanced at Schaeffer, then slid his gaze back to Prophet. "Ha!"

Schaeffer turned his head to one side, muttered something to the others, then kneed his black stallion ahead, until he was nearly directly below Prophet. He looked up at the bounty hunter.

"Lou Prophet, I take it?" he called amiably.

Prophet rolled the quirley between his lips and smiled.

"Your reputation precedes you."

Prophet shot a look across the canyon, pleased to see that Ronnie was staying out of sight, keeping his rifle where the sun couldn't reflect off the steel. "Eagle, you're ridin' with the wrong bunch," Prophet drawled.

Schaeffer smiled. He hadn't drawn a weapon, but he had one hand on the big Colt jutting from the cross-draw position on his left hip. "Why don't you go back to what you do best, Prophet? You'll find no bounties here."

"You got that wrong, Eagle. There're two big bounties on Crumb and Polk."

Crumb rose up in his stirrups and yelled angrily up the jagged canyon wall, "There are no bounties on my head!"

"Oh, yes," Prophet said with a slow nod. "For what you done to Bitter Creek, enslaving the whole town, intimidating and killing those who bucked you—I got a bounty on your head. And it's steep."

Prophet turned to Schaeffer. "Turn both men over to me, and I'll save you for another time and another place."

The Eagle smiled. The confidence in the smile and casual way the Eagle sat his horse made Prophet lift his gaze along the canyon wall opposite, just in time to see a shadow move out from between two boulders and level a rifle at Ronnie.

Raising his Winchester, Prophet dropped to a knee. "Kid, above you!"

21

THE GUNMAN ON the opposite canyon wall took Prophet's Winchester slug through his shoulder.

He spun around, dropping his rifle and slipping on the boulder he'd lighted on. With a shrill cry, he tumbled off the wall and plummeted like a potato sack to the canyon floor, landing with a crack and a grunt only a few feet before Schaeffer's horse.

"Proph!" Ronnie yelled.

The kid extended an arm to indicate something above and behind Prophet. The bounty hunter spun on his knee as a man in a bullet-crowned tan hat and blue shirt leapt onto a rock and crouched.

He extended a Spencer rifle with a stock trimmed with brass tacks, and fired.

Prophet had seen it coming and threw himself against the canyon wall. The gunman's slug sailed over Prophet's head, spanging off the trail below and setting several horses to whinnying.

Ronnie fired at the sharpshooter, but the slug smacked into an arrow-shaped rock partially shielding the man.

Prophet raised his Winchester and fired two rounds, levering quickly, watching the slugs thump into the gunman's chest, puffing dust from his shirt and blowing him back and out of sight.

Slugs slamming into the rocks and shrubs around him, Prophet hunkered down behind a boulder and peered at the trail below. The gunfire had startled the horses, throwing the gang into disarray. Several men were being flung about by their shrieking mounts. Others had taken cover behind rocks and shrubs and were firing at Prophet and at Ronnie on the opposite wall.

Schaeffer was yelling orders Prophet couldn't hear above the gunfire, whinnies, and clattering hooves.

He glanced above and around him, then scoured the opposite canyon wall. Seeing no other flanking riflemen, he glanced at Ronnie, nearly straight across the canyon, and allowed himself a taut smile.

The kid hunkered behind a rock, throwing lead down at the scattering gunmen, apparently unfazed by Schaeffer's two sharpshooters. His slugs had already pinked two gang members, one of whom was dragging a bloody leg toward a wild mahogany shrub, while another remained on hands and knees in the middle of the trail, head hanging sickly. As Prophet raised his rifle, the man was mowed over by a fleeing pinto and rolled into a yucca patch, limbs akimbo.

Prophet extended his Winchester and fired quickly, catching as many riders as he could still out in the open. Several slugs spanged off the rocks beside him, spraying shards.

He bolted behind the boulder to his left, peered around the other side, and continued shooting, levering the Winchester, taking hasty aim, and eliciting cries and curses from below.

When the Winchester clicked empty, he ducked back behind the rock and thumbed shells from his cartridge belt. Meanwhile, shooting resounded from the trail, and Ronnie was pounding away with his Sharps.

"They're tucked in too tight!" a man yelled from the trail.

"Pull out and—" His sentence was cut off and punctuated by a warbling shriek.

Prophet thumbed the last shell into the Winchester's breech, winced as a slug slammed into the rock a few inches from his face, then swung out from behind the rock, triggering two quick rounds while reconnoitering the trail.

The shooting had all but died, the bodies of two dead horses and several men littering the canyon floor.

Prophet lowered the Winchester and hunkered down, whipping his head around, looking for movement.

Silence. Smoke wafted around the canyon smelling like rotten eggs. Far off, a horse whinnied. Closer in but up the trail, a man groaned.

Prophet clamped down on what was left of his quirley and squinted at the opposite canyon wall. Ronnie poked his head out between two sharp-edged boulders, the rifle in his hands, his eyes round as saucers. As the kid moved farther out from between the rocks, a man in a checked shirt and tan vest rose from the slope just below him, raising a carbine where Ronnie couldn't see him.

Prophet snapped his Winchester up and shot the man through the base of the neck, slamming him against the slope. He lost his hat and carbine and rolled onto his back, slid feet-first several yards down slope before a boulder broke his fall, holding him there, straight up and down against the slope, chin resting on his chest.

A rifle popped in the heavy silence.

Hearing the slug whistle past his left ear, Prophet hunkered down and snapped his gaze across the canyon, where Ronnie stood, staring down his Sharps' smoking barrel.

A grunt sounded to Prophet's left.

He turned to see a mustachioed man stumble backward several steps, his rifle dropping in his right hand while his left rose to his chest. Blood shone beneath his black-gloved hand as he sat brusquely down on a rock and cursed. Thin lips drew back from his mouth, raising the waxed mustache and showing the small, yellow teeth and the gap where one was missing from the lower jaw.

"Fuck," Schaeffer said, his pale blue eyes twinkling in the west-angling sun. He didn't look at Prophet, but stared vacantly across the canyon, pain spoking his eyes. His voice was deep and strangled. "Tell me . . . tell me that ain't a kid that just shot me."

Prophet spit out the bits of paper and tobacco remaining from his quirley. "Well, he's eighteen. I reckon it depends on how you look at it. When I was eighteen . . . well, never mind."

Schaeffer sat there on the rock, wheezing and sighing and trying to plug the hole in his right center chest with his hand. It wasn't working. Blood ran down from beneath the glove, soaking his collarless, pin-striped shirt and doeskin vest.

Finally, the man's face bunched with fury. Cursing, he channeled the last of his remaining energy into his right hand, raising the rifle toward Prophet. He hadn't expected to get a shot off, however. It was just the way he wanted to go out.

Obliging the man, Prophet raised his own Winchester and drilled a round through Schaeffer's right temple, knocking his tan hat from his head and draping him back over the rock he'd been sitting on. The rifle fell against the rock, but remained in the Eagle's clenched fist for several seconds before the fingers slowly released it and it clattered onto the gravel.

Prophet whipped around to regard the canyon.

No more shooting. That didn't necessarily mean all the shooters were dead. A few could be hunkered down, waiting.

Seeing Ronnie making his way slowly down the opposite slope, a rifle in each hand, Prophet said without raising his voice, "Careful, boy."

Ronnie didn't look at him, just threw a hand up as he approached a dead man sprawled facedown over a shrub and kicked the man over with his right boot.

Prophet slowly made his way down the slope, investigating the bodies as he found them. All were dead or as good as dead.

He met Ronnie on the trail and began looking around for Crumb and Polk, finding Polk a hundred yards back up the trail, sprawled on his back with both hands pressed down on his gut. The trail showed scuff marks from where he'd dragged himself.

When Prophet's shadow fell across Polk's fair face, dark with two-day beard stubble, the druggist raised his head. He'd lost his hat and his domed forehead shone pale in the afternoon sun. Fear etched his gaze, and he panted.

The man gave a choked cry as Prophet squatted over him, patting him down for weapons. "Don't worry, Polk." He glanced at the man's torn guts, then raised his cold eyes to Polk's pain-clenched orbs. He stared hard, fighting the urge to finish the man. Better to let him lay here, let the bullet sear him and the vultures finish him off. "I'll leave you for the devil."

Prophet stood and began turning away to look for Crumb. Polk gasped. "Please . . . you can't just leave me. Help. . . ."

Ignoring the man, Prophet walked back into the canyon, and met Ronnie approaching from the opposite direction. "Any sign of Crumb?"

The kid threw up his hands. "No sign of him."

"And he wasn't on your slope?"

Ronnie shook his head.

His heart increasing its beat, Prophet looked around at the sprawled Jackrabbit riders and the three dead horses. Blood and viscera had been strewn around like spilled paint.

Chest clenching against the death smells, Ronnie voiced Prophet's own reluctant assessment. "He musta got away somehow. . . ."

He hadn't finished the sentence before Prophet began scrambling up the canyon's west wall, heading for the horses tethered on the other side of the ridge.

• • •

Henry Crumb clung to the saddle horn of the galloping dun, as though to a buoy in a storm-tossed sea.

The horse thundered across a salt lick, followed a bend in the narrow trail, and dipped into a swale fetid with a rotting deer carcass. Crumb grunted against the horse's left front shoulder, gritting his teeth as the horse's lunging gallop thrashed his organs like dice in a cup. The beast bolted up the opposite slope, barely slowing for the grade, and continued across the prairie, dusting the sage in its wake.

The horse continued hell-for-leather for another hundred yards. Then it started to blow and rasp and gradually stopped. Crumb felt the heavy, musky heat rising from its back. It turned quarter-wise with a heavy sigh, and Crumb looked through the gauzy brown dust sifting behind him, eyes spoked with fear.

Twenty minutes earlier, when the shooting had first started, bullets buzzing like angry bees around the canyon, Crumb had frozen in his saddle. He'd looked around in shock as bullets ripped through bodies, cracking bones and spraying blood. His head swam and his limbs turned to lead.

In spite of the iron grip he'd maintained on the town of Bitter Creek, no one had ever taken a shot at him. He'd never been physically assaulted in any way.

. He was, at heart, a timid albeit evil man who'd managed to keep his stranglehold on Bitter Creek and to keep making money. But the closest he'd ever come to using force was simply directing others, like Marshal Whitman and Dean Lovell, to do so. He'd never actually had to use his fists or his guns and wouldn't have known what to do had the need presented itself.

The gunfire had turned him to putty. Automatically, his knees had gripped the saddle of his skitter-hopping mount while his hands sawed back on the reins.

He'd felt the horse beginning to rear beneath him, and he clamped his jaws down hard, steeling himself. Just then a ricocheting slug slammed into a silver saddle ornament a half inch before his left knee. It twanged off the medallion, sparking and setting the horse to screaming.

Before Crumb knew what was happening, the horse was rocketing straight up the canyon trail.

Crumb slackened the reins and funneled all his energy into keeping his head low against the horse's neck, wrapping both hands around the saddle horn, and holding on. He didn't notice when his gray felt bowler blew off his head.

Eyes round with shock, he stared at the jagged line of rimrocks rising behind him, from which the breeze brought the pops and cracks of the rifle fire to his ears.

The two men Eagle Schaeffer had sent ahead of the main group, to reconnoiter the canyon and to foil the attack, were dead. Prophet and his cohort had the high ground. Even before Crumb had fled the canyon, the Jackrabbit riders were being ripped to shreds.

Crumb stared at the rimrocks, behind which the sun was slowly sinking, cloaking them in spruce-green shadows. The rifle fire died. Ten seconds later, two more reports sounded, then two more, and another.

Crumb stared toward the bloody canyon, mouth agape, his own blood draining from his face. He sat on the tired dun stony-eyed for several minutes.

Finally, he let the built-up pressure in his lungs escape in a slow sigh, and turned his gaze eastward, where the horse trail rose and fell over the tawny-green prairie toward Bitter Creek.

All was not yet lost. If he could get back to Bitter Creek ahead of Prophet, he could get his money from the safe in the depot station and give the town a parting gift it wouldn't soon forget. . . .

He reined the dun eastward and heeled it hard.

"Come on, ye son of a bitch. Move!"

22

IT WAS FULL dark when Henry Crumb trotted the dun along the outskirts of Bitter Creek. He halted the wary, sweat-lathered horse under a cottonwood and stared ahead at the night-shrouded Main Street lit dully by lights from the two saloons.

Finally, he reined the horse off the trail, wove a northern course amidst the cabins and scattered stables and privies, and drew rein in the alley behind the stage depot.

He climbed stiffly down from the saddle, threw his saddlebags over a shoulder, and spanked the dun's left hip. The exhausted mount stumbled forward a few steps and stopped, reins hanging, head drooping.

Crumb fished his keys from his pocket and unlocked the building's rear door. He stumbled inside, feeling his way down the dark hall, and turned through the low gate into the depot's main office. He tossed the saddlebags onto the floor near the Wells-Fargo safe hulking blackly against the room's east wall. When he'd gotten a lantern lit on the rolltop desk, he doffed his gloves, rubbed his hands together, and squatted down before the safe.

The lantern cast shadows about the room, illuminating the safe's silver-plated dial.

A sound rose behind the office door to Crumb's left.

He froze and turned to the door. Unholstering his revolver, he slowly turned the knob and gave the door a light shove, throwing it wide.

A short, dark silhouette stood before him, bulky in loose-fitting clothes, long black hair hanging about sloping shoulders. Crumb glanced left, saw the half-open window, the straw pallet, food tins, and bottles strewn about the floor. The smell of soup and stale sweat assaulted the mayor's nostrils. Someone had been living in the depot.

"Ay-eeeeeeeee!"

He was returning his gaze to the silhouette when the cry raked his ears.

The figure bounded toward him, slammed him back against the door frame. The fetid body odor thickened. As he struggled to regain his balance, sharp fingernails clawed at Crumb's face and neck, raking the skin. Red and white lights flashed behind his eyes.

Incensed by the pain, Crumb threw his left arm out savagely. Mad Mary screamed as she flew back against the desk. She half-turned, an animal-like warble growing up out of her throat, and leapt again toward Crumb.

She was three feet away when he thumbed back the hammer of his extended Colt and pulled the trigger.

Her scream changed pitch as she flew back against the desk, clung there for a moment, then rolled to the floor. She sobbed and grunted, kicking her legs.

Panting, feeling blood running down his face and neck, Crumb angled the Colt toward the half-breed whore and fired two more shots.

Mary gasped. Her left knee dropped. She lay quiet beneath the smoke webbing the darkness.

Crumb stared distastefully down at the unmoving form cloaked in darkness. Mad Mary was the first person he'd ever killed by his own hand. Repelled, he turned away, shook the fog from his head.

He glanced around anxiously. Had anyone heard the shots? He hurried to the two broad windows facing Main.

The only movement was two drovers leaving the American, wobbling slightly as they untied their horses from the rack and climbed unsteadily into their saddles, chuckling. Crumb released a breath, worry leaving him. In Bitter Creek, gunshots were no more cause for concern than barking dogs.

He holstered his pistol, hurried back to the safe, turned the dial a few times, and opened the heavy door. Quickly, he stuffed the bundled greenbacks and silver coins into the bags, dragged the bags to the front door, opened the door, looked cautiously up and down the street. Relieved to see that Prophet had not yet caught up to him, he headed west along the boardwalk.

A few minutes later, he returned to the depot station with a saddled piebald horse he'd taken from the rack before one of the brothels, and two five-gallon cans of kerosene he'd swiped from the mercantile, to which he had a key as he had a key to every business in town.

He retrieved the saddlebags from the depot building and heaved them over the horse, behind the saddle. It took him several minutes to position the horse at the north edge of town and then to dribble kerosene at a dozen strategic locations along Main, tossing lit matches as he went.

He'd made a complete circle and was back inside the depot station, tossing kerosene around the office, when the cries of "Fire! Fire!" rose in the west.

Crumb tossed the empty kerosene can into the room in which Mad Mary lay dead. Then he flicked a match alive on the telegraph key and tossed it into the glinting, snaking kerosene pool on the floor. .

The kerosene whooshed as it ignited. Crumb wheeled ahead of the ignition's hot wind, and he bolted out the depot's rear door, intending to sprint north to his horse. He'd taken only two steps, however, when a young man's voice rose to his left. "Hey!"

Crumb wheeled, saw a slender figure crouching there, a rifle in his hands. Crumb jerked his gun up and fired without aiming. He was surprised to hear the kid yelp and twist around, stumbling and falling as he clutched his right side.

As he crouched in the shadows behind the depot, Crumb's blood raced. Fear lanced him; his head reeled.

"Kid!" someone yelled.

Hooves pounded beyond the woodshed to Crumb's right, growing louder as they neared.

Cursing, he wheeled and ran back into the depot, heading for the front door. Flames leaped and wheeled around him. Smoke swirled, stinging his eyes and sucking the breath from his lungs. Holding an arm over his mouth, he fought the door open, bolted off the boardwalk, and ran, coughing, across the street.

"Crumb!"

He wheeled, bringing his pistol up, and fired at a tall, broad-shouldered figure galloping toward him on a snorting hammerhead from the west front corner of the depot station.

Prophet ducked as the pistol flashed, heard the bullet whistle to his left. He reined Mean to a skidding halt, raised his Winchester, and fired. His slug plunked into the grocery store as Crumb turned and ran into the shadows of the buildings along Main, shoes thumping along the boardwalk. Crumb was turning down an alley when Prophet levered the Winchester and fired again.

Crumb gave a shrill exclamation and disappeared down the alley.

Prophet lowered his rifle and turned to look behind him. The kid lay in the alley behind the station house, heaving onto his elbow while clutching his right side.

"I'm okay," Ronnie yelled, throwing up a hand. "Git that son of a bitch!"

Prophet gigged the horse forward slowly, peering east down Main, his jaw tightening. Flames leapt and roared from nearly every other building along both sides of the street. Smoke broiled from the windows and flame-lanced holes in the roofs, mushrooming toward the stars.

The saloons and cabins had emptied, and the citizens were scurrying about with water buckets, their shrill yells and shouted orders rising amidst the conflagration's roar. For a half second, Prophet considered helping, but there was no use. Crumb had set the fires so strategically that in a few minutes, the whole town would be engulfed.

Hearing the mercantile's windows shatter and rain onto the boardwalk as an explosion rocked the building, Prophet steadied his startled horse with a firm hand on the reins, and galloped down the dark alley after Crumb.

At the alley's end, he stopped, whipped his head right and left. Seeing nothing, he reined Mean left, trotting along the back of the buildings, peering down the smoke-choked space between each. When he'd ridden to the town's east end and seen nothing but burning buildings and the terrified citizens forming bucket brigades, he turned Mean back west down Main.

"Lou?"

He whipped his head around. Frieda was carrying a sloshing water bucket from a stock trough, her face streaked with soot. Handing the bucket to the town's blacksmith at the head of a bucket line before the harness shop, she whipped her exasperated gaze to Prophet.

"Crumb!" she cried, pointing her finger west. "He ran that way!"

Prophet put the steel to Mean, lunging west around the scurrying fire-fighters silhouetted against the toothy flames.

By now nearly every building was burning, burnishing

the night sky with a coppery glow. Several men and women had given up and stood looking around in shock; some slumped on stock troughs, some rested on knees in the street, holding handkerchiefs to their mouths.

Prophet whipped his head right and left, his rifle in his right hand. He came to the west edge of town, halted Mean, and stared off into the darkness beyond the burning town.

A gunshot snapped behind him. The slug whistled over his left shoulder. He ducked his head, whipped around, and extended the rifle out from his chest. Then he froze, heart leaping.

Crumb stood before the burning depot building, his head peeking out over the shoulder of young Ronnie Williams. The kid clutched his bloody right side with his left hand.

Crumb, who was Ronnie's height, stood just behind and slightly left of the boy, the barrel of his six-shooter pressed against the kid's right ear.

The orange flames leaping from the burning stage depot were reflected in both men's sweat-slicked faces. The heat from the flames caused their clothes to cling to their bodies. Prophet glanced beyond them, saw that the thick smoke concealed them from the other citizens concentrated on the other end of Main.

"Give me your horse!" Crumb shouted at Prophet. He thumbed his revolver's hammer back. "I'll kill him," he warned, poking the head against Ronnie's ear. The kid stretched his lips wide with a pained wince.

Prophet ran through his options, finding none that didn't get young Ronnie killed, except for turning Mean over to Crumb. He lowered the Winchester's barrel and climbed slowly, heavily out of the saddle.

"Lead it over here!" Crumb shouted above the roaring flames.

Prophet took two steps forward and extended the reins to Crumb, who shoved Ronnie aside. The boy fell in the dirt. As Crumb grabbed the reins, flames stabbed suddenly from the depot building's right front window. It took Prophet a half second to realize it wasn't flames. It was a giant, flaming bird, wings spread, burning head thrown back, blazing feathers showering sparks.

The bird gave a long, shrill cry as it dropped from the window and lighted on Henry Crumb's back.

"Ey-eeeeeeeeeeee!"

The cry cut through the fire's roar and caromed toward the stars.

Crumb slumped under the bird's weight, and he dropped his revolver. Flames from the burning bird showered the Bitter Creek mayor, setting his clothes on fire.

"Help me!" Crumb shouted, stumbling in circles, trying to shake the bird from his back. "Oh, God! Help me!"

Prophet stood frozen in place, watching the grisly spectacle, realizing the bird was Mad Mary and that her hands and legs had probably melted to the mayor by now.

Prophet knew there was nothing he could do to help either of them. Others, having heard Mary's shriek and Crumb's beseeching wails, came running through the smoke. They stopped when they saw the two people engulfed in flames, dancing a bizarre Virginia reel over the wheel ruts.

Finally, Crumb fell to his knees, every inch of his clothing now aflame, Mad Mary's arms wrapped around his neck, thighs clinging to his hips.

Crumb threw his head back and wailed incoherently. It was a deep, warbling cry rising above the thundering flames. Prophet and a half-dozen sweat-soaked, soot-streaked people stood in a semicircle around Crumb, who fell facedown in the street. Mary fell on top of him, still clinging to his back.

Blanketed in flames, both bodies lay still.

Bits of burning hair and clothes rose like cinders on the wind.

Prophet wrinkled his nose against the pungent smell,

and turned to Ronnie, half-reclining in the street. The kid's eyes were dark with pain.

Keeping his gaze on the boy, the bounty hunter said, "Someone get the sawbones!" He reached for the boy's arm. "Let's get you away from the fire."

"The town's finished, I reckon," Ronnie grunted miserably as Prophet led him west between burning facades, one arm slung over Prophet's neck.

The air was sooty and hot. Pine resin popped and sizzled as the flames jutted high against the sky. Beams collapsed, thundering and showering sparks.

"I reckon it depends on how you look at it," Prophet said, easing the kid along beside him. "Could be just the beginning."

EPILOGUE

PROPHET REMAINED IN Bitter Creek for a few days to help clean up after the fire.

To his surprise, most of the townspeople, including Frieda Schwartzenberger, decided to stay and rebuild and to run the town the way a town should be run—with a democratically elected mayor and town council and a marshal hired for the benefit of all. Bitter Creek was their home. They had nowhere else to go.

Only the businesses along Main Street had burned. Still, it would be a long rebuilding process. The night before Prophet decided to leave, a town council was elected. During the council's first meeting, held in Frieda's café, Ralph Carmody was elected mayor and his grandson, Ronnie Williams, recovering nicely from the bullet wound in his side, was named town marshal.

Prophet's going-away gift to the town was his reward money, found in Ralph Carmody's charred bank vault. The twenty-five hundred dollars, combined with the small fortune found on Henry Crumb's getaway horse, would give the town the financial boost it needed toward getting back on its own two feet.

Prophet's going-away gift to Frieda was a private, carnal love dance carried out under the second-story eaves of Gertrude's Good Food. A three-quarter moon slanted milky light through the window over the bed, limning Frieda's heels crossed over the small of the bounty-hunter's broad back.

Frieda's next-door neighbor—a widower farmer named Frank Roderus—was awakened three times in two hours by curious feral-like love screams carried on the wind. Thinking them only wild cats, he grunted, spit, and sank back onto his pillow.

Prophet was saddled up and riding the eastern trail from Bitter Creek when the sun rose from behind a hat-shaped rimrock and spread its pink light across the sage. Three hours later, he paused to let Mean draw water at a trailside spring. Suddenly, the dun raised its head and whinnied.

Prophet's hand touched his Colt while his eyes roamed the eastern horizon, finding a horseback figure silhouetted against the sky. The rider came on slowly. Prophet sat, his right hand caressing his pistol grips.

You never knew who you were going to run into out here. Prophet just hoped whoever it was wasn't trouble. He'd had enough trouble over the past few weeks. He wanted to go about his business unharassed, maybe wander down toward Glenwood Springs and wallow in the healing waters for a time.

As the rider approached, the lines around Prophet's eyes deepened gradually, the eyes themselves taking in the black Morgan and the female form of the rider, the ratty brown poncho, the long hair curving over slender shoulders, and the tan felt hat with chin strap.

She was fifty yards away when he muttered disbelievingly, "Louisa?"

Suddenly, she heeled the Morgan into a run. Mean

whinnied again and rippled his withers at the Morgan's familiar scent.

Prophet grinned as her haughty hazel eyes and dimpled chin came into focus. It really was her. He thought by now she'd be in Denver City. "Louisa."

Louisa reined the Morgan to a halt, neck-reining the black horse quarter-wise to Prophet and Mean. She furrowed her blond brows, pursed her rosebud lips, and placed one churlish fist on her hip. "Lou Prophet, where have you been?"

"Louisa, what in the name of the hounds of hell are you doin' out here?"

Her voice was matronly admonishing. "I sent telegram after telegram to Bitter Creek and received not one reply."

"The telegraph office was out of commission for a while."

"Don't tell me you've been in Bitter Creek this entire time!"

"Well, yeah, that's—"

She pooched her pink lips in disgust. "So you found a soiled dove and decided to while away a couple of weeks under the sheets?"

Prophet opened his mouth to object, but she cut him off. "Lou Prophet, you are the vilest, laziest creature the Good Lord set forth on this land. Living only to drink the devil's juice and couple with fallen women!"

Prophet found his ears warming like a scolded schoolboy's. "Louisa, that just ain't true. I been—"

Louisa slapped her hands to her ears. "Please don't assault me with the craven details!"

Prophet glared at her. "Louisa, I'm trying to tell you, I been—"

She squeezed her eyes shut. "Please stop!"

Finally, he sighed and leaned over his saddle horn, jutting his chin and screwing up his eyes. "Louisa," he shouted, "would you please just tell me what in the hell you're doin' here!"

She removed her hands from her ears and opened her eyes. "When I couldn't contact you through the telegraph from Denver City, I decided to start scouring the country-side for you. Bitter Creek was the last place I saw you."

He grinned, happy to see her, churlish as she was. "So, now you found me. What's up?"

"We have a job to do, Lou Prophet. It's a big job. Too big for me alone."

Prophet shook his head. "No jobs for me. Not for at least a month. I'm wrung out."

"I told you I didn't want to hear the details of your devil party."

He started to snarl a rebuttal, but again she cut him off. "Quit horsing around, Lou. We have trouble in the South-west." She reined the Morgan around and canted it back the way she had come. "Come on," she yelled behind her. "I'll tell you about it on our way to Cheyenne!"

"Cheyenne?" Prophet snorted.

"We'll pick up the train there!"

"Train?"

Prophet glared at her bobbing back. Finally, he shook his head, kneed Mean into a trot, and yelled, "Louisa, you're a caution—you know that?"

He sighed and cursed and patted Mean's neck. "No rest for the weary, Mean. Not when that girl's anywhere within three territories . . ."

Grudgingly, he galloped Mean and Ugly into Louisa's sifting dust.

Peter Brandvold was born and raised in North Dakota. He's lived in Arizona, Montana, and Minnesota, and he currently resides in the Rocky Mountains near Fort Collins, Colorado. Since his first book, *Once a Marshal,* was published in 1998, he's become popular with both readers and critics alike. His writing is known for its realistic characters, authentic historical details, and lightning-fast pace. Visit his website at www.peterbrandvold.com. Send him an e-mail at pgbrandvold@msn.com.

"MAKE ROOM ON YOUR SHELF OF FAVORITES
FOR PETER BRANVOLD."
—FRANK RODERUS

THE DEVIL GETS HIS DUE
A LOU PROPHET NOVEL BY
PETER BRANVOLD

On the trail with Louisa Bonaventure,
"The Vengeance Queen," bounty hunter Lou
Prophet is caught in a bloody crossfire of hatred
between an outlaw who would shoot a man dead
for fun and Louisa, who has sworn to kill him—
even if she dies trying.

"THE NEXT LOUIS L'AMOUR."
—ROSEANNE BITTNER

0-425-19454-X

PE... C106608051 ...D

ONCE A MARSHAL   0-425-16622-8

The son of an old friend rides into Ben's life with a plea for justice and
a mind for revenge. The boy suspects rustlers have murdered his
rancher father, and the law is too crooked to get any straight answers.
Can the old marshal live up to the role of legendary lawman the boy
has grown up to admire?

ONCE MORE WITH A .44   0-425-17556-1

Ben Stillman returns to Clantick, Montana Territory, to clean up a
town that's gone wild and dirty since he left it.

ONCE A LAWMAN   0-425-17773-4

Stillman thought he'd finished dispensing hard justice in the town of
Clantick. But then a courtesan and her latest client are found dead
with their throats slit, and Stillman must track down the killer.

ONCE HELL FREEZES OVER   0-425-17248-1

A vicious gang of murdering outlaws have taken refuge from the brutal
cold of winter in a neighboring mountain cabin—taking everyone
inside hostage. It's Sheriff Ben Stillman's duty to save them. But the
hardened lawman is taking this personally—and for good reason: they
have his wife, too.

ONCE A RENEGADE   0-425-18553-2

Sheriff Ben Stillman has a murder on his hands—but there's no one
better at tracking down a bloodthirsty killer.